JUST AS I Am

BELOVED & ENOUGH

LETA BUHRMANN

To Galen, my coach and friend.
Thank you for your wisdom, guidance, and support. Your
ability to ask the right questions helped open my soul to hear
God's voice and is helping me become the woman
I was created to be.

A NOTE TO MY READERS:

This book contains material that may be triggering for individuals who have experienced trauma. It specifically references rape and domestic violence. If you have experienced trauma and find this material triggering, I urge you to take care of yourself and your mental health.

If you are in distress, please reach out for help and call 988. The 988 lifeline provides free and confidential support, 24/7.

Chapter 1

THE PHONE CALL I HAD RECEIVED from my former business partner haunted my thoughts long after our conversation ended. I found myself restless with no real reason, and distressing emotions I thought I had dealt with from my past were back too. They surfaced soon after the call. Though I had spent the last year addressing a lifetime of trauma and had made significant progress, it suddenly felt like I was back at the beginning of my recovery journey.

The call had hit me like a punch in the stomach. For reasons I didn't understand, disorienting feelings of gloom now hovered over me like a dark cloud, but I couldn't identify exactly why I was feeling this way. I felt adrift in an ocean of hopelessness, unmoored to anything solid. Even my old fears of being abandoned and feeling unlovable were creeping up on me. I had made considerable progress in recovering from my trauma over the last year, and the return of these feelings and fears terrified me. My faith had become very important to me during my recovery, and I wondered what this regression in my journey meant. Was something wrong with me? Was my faith weak? Were my healing and my renewed faith simply delusions I told myself to feel better? How could something as innocuous as a phone call from a former business partner cause such unease? How could it get under my skin and work its way to my soul?

I drifted aimlessly through the house as I tried to decide what specifically bothered me. Instead of clarity, I found only confusion, so I decided to wander outside. Anytime I felt anxious or distracted, I felt drawn to my small apple orchard. The trees brought comfort to me. I strongly felt God's presence when I was in nature, but I especially felt His nearness in this orchard. Peace—yes, God's peace was what I always felt there. My grandparents had planted the trees decades earlier, and as a child I would spend hours there. I often climbed the trees as high as I could and sat there reading a book. Even as an adult, I loved to sit beneath a tree and simply breathe in nature. It wasn't only the closeness of God's presence that I found there. The trees also helped me center myself.

My business partner and I had operated a law firm that represented special interest groups before Congress. After my grandmother's death not quite a year ago, I had turned over my interests in the business when I decided to relocate to what had been my grandparents' farm. I inherited the farm after my grandmother's death, and that continued to amaze me. I had never planned to own a farm. In fact, I never dreamed I would want to move back to my childhood home.

I had been raised on this farm by my grandparents after my parents were killed in a car accident. Although I knew my grandparents and extended family loved me, my pain prevented me from feeling their love. For years, I tied my pain from several traumatic events to this farm and to my past in general. When I finally left for college, I left my past, this farm, and my family behind—that was, until the day I received the phone call telling me that my grandmother did not have long to live, and I came home to say goodbye to her. After her death, I experienced a spiritual awakening, and I eventually decided to permanently relocate to the farm my family had owned for generations. Life can be filled with surprising twists and turns.

My former business partner had called to inform me that he had decided to follow my lead and begin a new chapter in his own life. He had decided to close the business we had founded to join the biggest lobbying firm in the city. I was shocked by his decision. In a way, I guess I felt betrayed. Even though I had chosen to leave, I thought the business would continue. It felt like a part of me, something I had helped create, had died.

When my former partner told me about his new job, he only talked about his huge salary. He didn't talk about less stress or having the time to work on projects that interested him. I'm not sure what bothered me more, that he had closed the business or that he was going to be making an absurd amount of money. When I relocated, I told myself a big salary wasn't important to me anymore. I thought that working for myself and utilizing my legal degree to help my neighbors and friends through their legal problems was what I wanted and what I felt called to do. A true purpose, instead of money, was what I was seeking. Now, however, my income was so small that I couldn't afford to rent an office. I was working from a bedroom in my farmhouse. I asked myself over and over—if money wasn't important to me, then why did the call bother me? Was I jealous? Was I doubting my decisions? Was I concerned with the ramifications of my former partner's decision on the other employees? Question upon question flew through my mind.

The thought I kept coming back to was doubt, but I couldn't

quite describe why. Was I doubting my decisions, or was it something deeper? His call certainly reminded me of everything I had left behind. Did I miss the power and prestige of my former career? And why had this call reignited the old nightmares and fears from my past? Something deep had been triggered within me, but I couldn't explain or understand it.

In the orchard, I sat under one of the larger trees and prayed. I needed to feel the dirt under me and the tree behind me as I leaned into it. Answers would not come today. I already sensed that. Eventually, I laid flat on the grass and looked up into the trees. Even though they had only a hint of buds at this time of year, I was already looking forward to the cool shade these trees would provide in the summer. It was one of the few places on the farm that provided a refreshing place to take a break from the never-ending work list. Of course, there was also the connection to my grandparents here. Now that they were both gone, I cherished this physical reminder of them. I took a deep breath to quiet my mind and thought about my grandmother. I wondered what wisdom she would have had about this phone call.

Suddenly I heard someone calling my name with urgency in her voice. It was Aunt Lu, my widowed aunt who had moved in with my grandmother after her husband, Uncle Vern, died. Because of my aunt's care over the years, my grandmother was able to remain in her home until she died. When my grandmother died and I inherited the farm, I asked my aunt to continue living in the house with me. It was a big house with a large garden, and it was too much work for one person to live in and care for. Besides, my aunt was the best cook I had ever met, and my culinary skills were lacking. So far, our unique living arrangement had worked well for both of us.

I jumped up from my spot under the tree. "I'm over here in the orchard," I yelled.

"Lydia, I've been hollering myself hoarse. Didn't you hear me?"

"I'm so sorry, Aunt Lu. I guess I was so deep in thought that I didn't hear anything but my own thoughts."

Aunt Lu looked at me with genuine concern. "Honey, are you okay? You have not seemed like yourself the last couple of days. To be honest, you seem as tense and stressed as when you first came back home."

"I guess I have been a bit preoccupied," I admitted.

Aunt Lu looked at me, waiting for me to say something else, but I didn't know what else to say. How could I explain what I was feeling when I didn't understand it myself?

When I didn't add anything else to my explanation, Aunt Lu continued. "You've had a couple of phone calls today. Sam and Gail both called, and they both asked you to call them back."

"Of course. I will do that in just a bit. I want to take a walk first to get some exercise."

Aunt Lu looked at me intently, but she simply nodded and went back to the house.

Exercise. That was exactly what I needed. Perhaps if I burned off some energy, it would help clear my mind. One of the benefits of quiet country roads was that you could take a walk and not worry about traffic. After I moved back to the farm, I gained a bit of weight because of Aunt Lu's amazing cooking. I began feeling sluggish and out of sorts, so I started walking and occasionally running to feel better. I had lost some of those pounds, but more importantly, I felt better.

Aunt Lu's observation that I seemed as stressed and tense as I had when I first moved back to the farm was upsetting. I did not want to revert to that version of myself. That version felt broken. Before moving to the farm, I had never faced the past traumas of my life, and those things had built and built upon each other. It had taken me years to recognize and admit that I was a survivor of date rape. The shame of that experience led me to repeatedly make poor decisions in my life, especially regarding relationships. With each new relationship, I had convinced myself that I was in love, and each time, I repeated making the same poor choices. My self-loathing, guilt, and shame grew with each broken relationship.

When I moved back to the farm, I was a bitter and broken woman. I had shut out everyone who loved me. I had spent years running from my past and from God. I blamed God for my pain and for not protecting me, and I was convinced I was unlovable. But then, I experienced what I describe as a spiritual transformation. It took time and help from others, but I realized that God doesn't love people like people love people. I learned that I cannot earn, or lose, God's love. I realized that God's redemption was for me even though I had experienced trauma. It had taken prayer, time, work, and tears, but I liked the woman I was becoming. For the first time in years, the reflection I saw in the mirror was of a woman who was not filled with shame but with peace. I did not want to slip back into the old version of myself.

I realized I had walked so far on this quiet country road that I had better head home before I was too exhausted to make it. Even though I had not resolved any of my thoughts, I was full of fresh air and the exercise had tired me. Tomorrow I would think more about how to resolve this turmoil that swirled around me.

The next morning, I joined Aunt Lu in the kitchen and poured myself a cup of coffee, made some toast, and then sat down at the table. Our kitchen still looked exactly as it had when I was a child. It was retro before retro was popular. My grandmother had never wanted a dishwasher or a microwave and neither did my aunt. Since Aunt Lu did all the cooking, I hadn't pushed the issue. My favorite part of this "retro" kitchen was the antique table. It could fold down to take up less space, but I don't remember it ever having been folded. We were always ready to feed one more mouth at our table. The opened table and Aunt Lu's wonderful cooking guaranteed we were always ready.

When I sat down, Aunt Lu left the sink of dishes, dried her hands, and sat down with me. "Will you please tell me what's wrong?" she asked. "You've been preoccupied for long enough."

I sighed and then told her, "I received a call from my old business partner. He closed our business and took a job with another firm. I can't get that call out of my mind. I'm upset about it, and I'm not sure why. Everything I tell myself to explain my feelings doesn't seem like the real reason, and I can't seem to pinpoint the true source."

Aunt Lu listened and nodded. I had the feeling she wanted to say something but could not bring herself to voice it. Then she finally said, "It sounds like you have thoughts and feelings to sort out. I've always found it helpful to talk to a trusted friend about difficult topics. It seems to me you and Gail have that type of friendship."

She stood, patted my arm, and added, "Why don't you call her after you help me with all of these dishes?"

I laughed and said, "Work before play. I get it."

"I've also learned that doing a little work often helps me think better. I thought it might help you as well. Besides, did you see that pile of dishes? I will be here all day."

Once we finished cleaning up the kitchen, I took my aunt's advice and called Gail. Aunt Lu was correct that Gail was a trusted friend. In my grandmother's words, Gail was my dear *soul friend*. We talked about everything – the mundane and the deep. Our friendship was based on trust, and it allowed us to share our most personal pain and traumas. Gail was the history teacher at our local high school, and we also attended the same church. In fact, that was where I first met her. It wasn't long after my grandmother's funeral when Gail approached me at church and asked if I would speak to one of her classes. She wanted me to "make some of the governmental and political information come to life." I don't know if I accomplished that in my speech, but I used my years of working in Washington, DC, to include details that I hoped would make the material more interesting to the students. They seemed pleased to listen to me, so maybe I had been successful.

In the time Gail and I had known each other, we had frequently discussed our personal struggles. She was the first person I told that I was a rape survivor. And she shared with me the stories of her struggles in school when she was a girl. After years of difficulties with learning and the resulting lack of self-esteem, one of her teachers realized that what others had labeled as failure was actually a learning challenge. That teacher's compassion for her students and passion for teaching led Gail to follow in her footsteps.

Gail was the most passionate educator I had ever met. She also had a challenging childhood outside of school. Though her parents each showed their love to her in their own ways, their marriage was fraught with fighting. She witnessed their arguments, and this trauma tainted her early years. As an adult, Gail had read books, spent time praying, and had worked with a therapist to help her find peace in her life. I was blessed that she shared what she had learned with me. She was unquestionably my soul friend.

Chapter 2

GAIL AND I ADMITTED that we had both hibernated a bit during the harsh winter weather, and it had been too long since we had dinner together. Although spring had not yet officially arrived, the weather was finally a bit warmer. We decided to celebrate surviving the cold months by driving to our favorite locally owned steak restaurant. Our conversation on the thirty-minute drive was mostly about the weather, and we laughed about how we sounded like a couple of old ladies complaining that the cold hurt our bones.

Our conversation remained lighthearted as we enjoyed our delicious meal. When we couldn't eat another bite, we started to catch up on serious conversations. Gail filled me in on the classes she was teaching and the material each class was learning.

"My friend, you continue to amaze me with how passionate you are about your profession. I'm so happy you found your true calling. And look at the students you are impacting. You may never know what seeds you are planting," I told her.

"That's one of the things I love about teaching. I love seeing the proverbial light bulb moment when a student grasps a new concept, and I also love knowing that, as you said, I'm planting seeds. I know some of my students have never heard a positive word before, so I try to find something to praise about each of them. I hope they know that I appreciate them just for who they are."

I nodded with appreciation for her passion.

"Now, enough about me. You seem preoccupied, Lydia. What's going on with you?"

I told her about the phone call from my former business partner. I confessed how it had bothered me, and how this nagging sense of doubt that I couldn't pinpoint hovered over me.

"Are you doubting your decision to leave your previous career and move back here?" she asked.

"I don't know what I'm thinking. Why would this bother me to this degree if I had made the right decision?"

"It does sounds like you might be doubting things, but doubt does not mean your decision was wrong. I think you need to dig in and discover what it is precisely that you are doubting. I'm sorry, my friend, but you also mentioned the large salary he was offered. Is it possible that this is simply jealousy?"

"Wouldn't you question your decisions if you realized a different path could have led to a huge salary? I mean, I'm working as hard as I ever have, and yet I'm not earning much of a paycheck. Not even enough to afford an office."

"I think that depends on your priorities. Is money your main focus? I didn't think it was. I thought your priorities had changed when you made the decision to move back here. Money and power were replaced with peace and purpose. Has that changed for you? Just because the world says something should be our priority doesn't mean that is accurate. The world's priorities can be a lie to us.

"You must sort this out and decide over and over what is truly important to you. It can be a battle when your priorities conflict with what the world says your priorities should be, but it is a battle worth fighting. You will have to put in the work to decide what is important to you. And you will also have to put in the work to decide if there is something deeper bothering you.

"And speaking of putting the work in, there is something else on my mind. You've seemed so tired lately when I've seen you at church. I've wondered if your workaholic tendencies have resurfaced. I know you just said you aren't making money, but please consider whether the hours you are working are because you need the money or if they're because you are avoiding something. Those old ways can sneak back in on us, and before we know it, they are in control of us again." Gail paused for emphasis and then said, "Okay, I will stop. I know I've thrown several things out there, but I also know you are good at self-reflection. I've just given you material to consider."

I sipped my water and let all this sink in. In the past, I would have been offended by someone challenging me and questioning me in this way, but I had learned that this is what soul friends do for each other. These questions and this honest conversation were exactly what I needed as I continued to think about what was bothering me about that call.

"Thank you for your honesty and your advice. As you said, you've given me much to consider," I told her.

"That's what friends are for, and I'm thankful for our friendship."

With our stomachs full and my mind already pondering our conversation, we ended our dinner. As was typical for me after having deep conversations with Gail, I spent the remainder of the evening in silence. My soul was mulling over what we had discussed. Perhaps I had not had any revelations yet, but I knew I was on the correct path to insight.

Gail's comment that I needed to put in work to decide what was important to me made sense. After a restless night of sleep, I decided the best way to put in the work was through prayer and journaling my thoughts. I had discovered in the last year that journaling was the best method for me to process the thoughts swirling in my mind. It also seemed that writing allowed me to hear God's wisdom for me. Perhaps that was because I silenced distractions so I could focus on writing. I grabbed my notebook and pen and sat down at my writing desk. Just like the rest of the furniture in this room, the desk had been here since my childhood. Even though I had moved away years ago, Grandmother had left everything as it was, waiting for me to return. It was a comfort to realize that some things stayed the same even when most of your life was changing before your eyes.

Where do you begin when you are questioning everything? I started by telling God I needed help.

"God, I'm sitting here at another potential crossroad. I feel that I made a grave mistake taking this path."

I felt God asking me why I thought my current path was a mistake. Before I could answer, I clearly heard God ask me if the life I left brought me peace and joy. And who was I serving on that path?

A strong feeling came to me, and I began to write.

God, I feel so confused about my decisions and myself. I feel lost. Ungrounded. And I feel that something is missing, but I don't know what it is.

Something was missing. It seemed that I was getting closer to the root of why the phone call was bothering me. I wasn't sure why the feeling of something missing was important, but I knew this was a topic that I needed time to process.

I leaned back in the chair and thought about what I had sensed and written, and I wondered if it represented a conversation with God. If the voice of God could be described as the still, small voice within, then I was sure it was. In the past when I felt that a message came from God, I had an amazing sense of peace. It was a peace that transcended all understanding and description. I smiled. Yes, I felt that peace. It appeared God had provided me with topics that needed to be explored. I wrote nothing else, but I knew these topics would remain on my mind for quite some time.

Chapter 3

MY MIND HAD BEEN SO PREOCCUPIED that I had not yet talked to Sam about the upcoming planting season. Sam Harmon had farmed for Grandmother when she was alive, and I was thankful he had been willing to continue in that role when I inherited the farm. Sam was three years older than me, and we had gone to school together. In fact, we were on the same bus route.

We seemed to have an attraction to each other, but because of my history with bad relationships, I was hesitant to pursue a new one. Sam had not made any first moves either, so perhaps the attraction was only in my mind. Gail had recommended I not begin any relationship until I had focused on healing, and I thought that was good wisdom. Since I still didn't feel comfortable pursuing a relationship, I thought that might be a sign I still had healing to do. But I wondered how long my healing would take.

One year. It occurred to me that I had moved back to the farm a year ago. That meant my grandmother had died a year ago as well. I couldn't believe an entire year had passed. I didn't want that first year to be over yet. There was still grieving to do. Society seemed to stress the first year after the death of a loved one. The implication seemed to be that after the one-year anniversary, you should move beyond the grief. Having lived through that year, I knew that was ridiculous. It was simply not enough time to work through the grief of losing someone you loved.

That was especially true when there were multiple layers to the grief. I grieved for my grandmother, but I also grieved because I had isolated myself from my family and my past for so long. That was a coping mechanism I had used to avoid facing my trauma. In the long run, it caused my pain to increase. By not processing the trauma, it continued to torture me. And the isolation kept me away from my loved ones. I had also learned that new grief often awakens past grief. Even though my parents and grandfather had died years ago, the death of my grandmother brought back the pain of those long-ago losses.

My thoughts drifted back to Sam. I mentioned to Aunt Lu that I needed to catch up with Sam about farm business, and she suggested I invite him to Sunday dinner. I wasn't sure if she was trying to play matchmaker or was simply wanting an opportunity to cook for an army. When I called Sam, he was thrilled to be invited because he knew the feast that would await him.

As expected, when Sunday arrived, Aunt Lu prepared a feast: fried chicken, mashed potatoes, green beans, rolls, and not just one, but two kinds of pie.

"Aunt Lu, did you invite the entire church over for dinner?" I asked.

"No, dear, why do you ask?"

"There's enough food here for at least ten people. You do realize there will only be three of us, don't you?"

"I plan to send Sam home with leftovers. I know that young man does not cook for himself. He's just bones."

What could I do but smile? Aunt Lu's love language was

cooking. I had yet to meet a person who would say no to her love. She was without a doubt the best cook I had ever met.

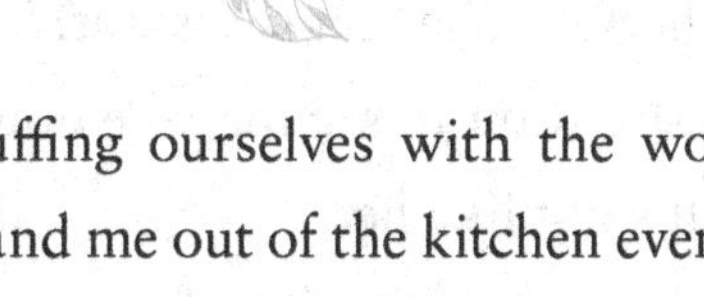

After we finished stuffing ourselves with the wonderful meal, Aunt Lu kicked Sam and me out of the kitchen even though it left her to wash dishes by herself. I asked Sam if he would like to take a walk. He thought that sounded like a good idea since he had filled himself with so much food. Aunt Lu winked at me, and I shot her a pleading look that said *please don't say anything*. She grinned and returned to cleaning up as we left.

"How about a stroll to the orchard?" I suggested when we stepped outside.

"Sounds like a great idea. How have things been going around here? I haven't seen you lately."

"Oh, everything is fine here. I've been preoccupied with a few things, but they aren't of importance. How are you? Anything new with the farm?"

"The farm's fine," he answered.

I waited for him to continue, but he didn't. We walked on in silence until I pushed the topic again. "Okay. I'm glad to know the farm is fine, but you didn't answer about yourself. How are *you* doing?"

Sam stopped walking and looked at me. For a minute, I thought I saw a tear in his eye until he blinked it away. Maybe it had just been my imagination, but something urged me to stay quiet and wait for him to speak. He was usually a very private man, and I didn't want to pry if he didn't want to talk.

Finally, he said, "Lydia, there's something wrong with Ellie."

"Your sister?"

"Yeah. I don't know what's going on, but something is wrong."

"What causes you to think that?" I asked.

"She's not herself. She seems distant. She doesn't want me to come over, doesn't want to see me. She doesn't even want to talk on the phone. It's not like her."

Ellie had been two years ahead of me in school, but I knew her. We weren't friends growing up because she was older than me and we had very little in common, but I had always liked her. She had loved fashion and looking her best, but I didn't have any interest or skill in those areas. She had also been a cheerleader and went on to marry her high school sweetheart not long after they graduated. He was a very good athlete in school, and as I recalled, he knew it! It had always seemed strange to me that she was attracted to him. She was a very kind person, but he was an arrogant jerk.

"Is there anything I can do?" I asked.

"You have a way of talking to people. You make people feel comfortable, and they share stuff with you. And you always seem to be able to sense when something is wrong. Would you talk to her and see if you think I'm right? Maybe I'm just imaging that something's wrong."

"Don't you think it would be odd if I just called her out of the blue and asked her what was new? I haven't talked to her in years."

Sam sighed and stared at the ground. Finally, he looked up and simply said, "Can't you think of something?"

I felt such a tender rush of emotions toward him. He was obviously very concerned about his sister. I took a deep breath.

"I will think of something," I said.

Relief washed over his face immediately. "Thank you, Lydia. Thank you."

He opened his mouth to say something else, but the words appeared to be caught in his throat. He looked at the ground again. When he looked up, all he said was, "Tell Lu I said thanks for lunch. I gotta go."

Sam hurried away, and I was left alone with my thoughts. What had he been trying to say before he left? And what could be so wrong with his sister that he couldn't even visit for very long? Ellie always seemed to have it all together. In high school, she had a large circle of friends. She was a caring person, and people were drawn to her. She was also very pretty, and I wondered if perhaps part of that came from her kind and caring personality shining outward. Walking back to the house, I struggled with ideas about how to reach out to her without it being forced or awkward. That was going to be a challenge because I always seemed to be awkward in these situations.

After agonizing about what to do, I finally decided to call Ellie and just come right out and invite her over. I prayed that I would sound natural and not forced.

When she answered, I stumbled over my words. "Um, hi, this is Lydia Roberts. Is this Ellie?"

She responded, "Yes, it is."

"I don't know if you remember me, but—"

Before I could finish my sentence, she responded, "Yes, I remember you."

Though she didn't say it, I imagined Ellie wondering why I was calling her after all these years, so I began trying to explain. "I moved back here a year ago, and I would love to connect with more people." Then, I paused awkwardly. The silence continued, and since I felt uncomfortable, I started talking again. "I was accustomed to being around people where I worked before I moved back, and I recently realized I've been feeling isolated. My aunt Lu had a church directory, and I found your number. So, anyway, I was wondering if you'd like to come over to my house for coffee sometime."

She took a minute, but she said, "Sure. I could come over for coffee."

"Wonderful! When would work for you? My schedule is flexible."

"What about tomorrow morning? I could be there around nine."

I was surprised she agreed since she took a while to respond, and I was even more surprised when she suggested the next day. Somehow, I was able to blurt out, "That's great. I will see you tomorrow."

I fretted all afternoon about what to talk about and how I would learn if there was something troubling her. I couldn't simply blurt out, "Your brother is terribly worried about you." To take my mind off the conversation, I decided to make a coffee cake to serve with our coffee. Aunt Lu came into the kitchen when she heard me banging the pots and pans around.

"Lydia, do you need any help?" she asked.

"I'm looking for the nine-inch cake pan. Sam's sister, Ellie, is coming over tomorrow, and I thought a coffee cake would be nice."

Aunt Lu smiled. "Yes, it would. All the cake pans are over here. Do you need a recipe?"

I looked down at the floor and sighed. "Yes, that would be good."

Aunt Lu smiled again and headed over to the counter where she kept her enormous box of recipes. "It's so nice you invited her over. I'm glad you're making friends. You should spend time with people other than just your old aunt," she said as she looked through her recipe cards.

"I don't know what I would do without you," I told her. "I can't even find what I need in the kitchen. I must admit, I'm a little nervous about inviting Ellie over. She was always one of the popular girls in high school, and I was never in her group."

"Oh, honey, high school is over. We are all just people doing the best we can. I suspect Ellie might be a bit nervous spending time with you. Here's my favorite coffee cake recipe. Do you want me to help you with it?"

I took a deep breath and replied, "No, but thank you. I want to do this."

"Just call me if you need me."

She handed me the index card, and I got to work, trying to focus on the recipe and not my nerves. I stopped occasionally while measuring the ingredients and wondered if Aunt Lu was right. Would Ellie be nervous too? I wondered why one of the popular girls would be nervous spending time with me.

Ellie was still as pretty as I remembered. When I greeted her at the door the next afternoon, I noticed that her hair and makeup were both perfect. I hoped I had remembered to brush my hair.

"Hi, Ellie. Welcome. Is it okay if we sit in the kitchen? I believe Aunt Lu is in the living room reading the paper, and I think our chatting might distract her."

"The kitchen is fine with me," Ellie replied.

While Ellie was still pretty and stylish, I also noticed there was something different about her: there seemed to be sadness in her eyes. She followed me to the kitchen, but she didn't say anything. I had the sense that I would be leading this conversation. As I poured coffee for both of us, I tried to think of something to say. My mind was blank, and Ellie still hadn't said anything, so I did the only thing I could think of. I silently prayed for help to know what to say.

I put the coffee cake and our mugs on the table. Since we were both still standing, I gestured to a chair and said, "Please, have a seat." After we both sat down, I paused for another moment and then jumped in. "Thank you so much for coming over. Like I told you when I called, I haven't connected with very many people since I moved back. When I mentioned to Aunt Lu that I had invited you, she was pleased. She thinks I should spend time with more people than simply her."

Ellie took a sip of coffee and said, "I have to say, Lydia, I think everyone is still surprised you made the decision to move back here. I mean, this place is very boring compared to the life you used to live."

"Ah, well, frequently what seems exciting ends up not being that wonderful after all. It took me coming back here and doing a great deal of soul searching and praying to come to that difficult conclusion."

Ellie put her cup down and said with disdain, "Praying."

She looked off in the distance. I knew that look. She was trying to decide if she wanted to say something. This time I let the silence grow.

She finally added, "I haven't been to church in a while."

She didn't add to her statement. Should I say something? What could I say?

I finally asked, "Why is that?"

"Oh, you don't want to hear my stories. They're too dull to mess with."

"Quite the opposite. I think people's stories are always interesting."

Ellie picked up her cup again and took another sip. "Not mine."

After another period of silence that was becoming uncomfortable, I decided to take the conversation in a different direction.

"Do you still see anyone that was in your class?" I asked.

She seemed grateful for the subject change. "You can't help but see people in this small community. Not everyone was able to move away. Most stayed right here."

I was taken aback by her comment. Was she insinuating something about me? How should I respond?

Ellie must have sensed my discomfort, because she quickly said, "I'm so sorry, Lydia. I didn't mean anything by that. I guess it's been so long since I've socialized, I don't even know how to behave."

"Oh, no worries. I know it's strange that I left for years and then came back. I'm guessing that caught many people off guard."

"It's just that some of us always thought we would be like you and move away, and then, well . . . I guess life happens."

"Yes, it does. Often not as we expect."

Ellie nodded her agreement. After another pause, she continued, "I need to go. I have some errands I need to run.

Thank you for the coffee cake and coffee. I've enjoyed catching up with you."

"Same here, Ellie. Maybe we could do this again."

"Sure." She paused for a moment and then looked me in the eye. "That would be nice."

After she left, I texted Sam, who knew I was having coffee with her. He stopped by later that day.

"Well?" he asked without even a greeting.

I chuckled. "Wow, Sam. I can tell you don't want any small talk today!"

"Not when my sister's well-being is being discussed. What did she say? What do you think is going on?"

"Honestly, she didn't say much. I don't know if it's because we haven't spoken in so long or whether she's hiding something. She basically answered in one-word sentences. However, I do have one bit of good news: she agreed to meet again. I will wait a few days and then call her back."

Sam sighed. "I was hoping she would confide in you."

"Look, she and I are basically strangers. We haven't seen each other in years. It takes time to build trust where someone is comfortable sharing problems."

"I suppose that's true."

"Let's say some prayers and have some patience. We can view this time as planting seeds of friendship."

"You're right. I will pray. And although I generally have patience, I am afraid this is one time when that will be a struggle. I will do my best."

"That's all any of us can do," I said.

Sam left to get back to work. Spring was nearing, which meant it would soon be planting season, and he needed to make sure the equipment was ready. I decided to inspect the flower beds to make sure they would be ready as well. As I cleaned out a few dead leaves and cut down some weeds that had already begun to grow, I thought about my time with Ellie. It was too difficult to guess what was going on. She did seem to be holding back on something, but I kept reminding myself that I was like a stranger to her. Then there were her comments that not everyone moved away, and some people thought they would move but didn't.

I decided not to spend time thinking about it. Instead, I would focus on getting to know her better and praying that if something was wrong, she would begin to feel comfortable and share that with me.

Chapter 4

REVEREND PETERS HAD BEEN THE PASTOR of our church for several years. He led my grandmother's funeral service the previous year, and I still remembered his message. He shared a conversation he had with her in the weeks leading up to her death. Grandmother told him she'd been rocking in her chair and talking to Jesus. It was very moving when he said we all could have that type of comforting, talking-to-a-dear-friend relationship with Jesus. It felt as if he had written his message specifically for me because at the time, my soul was still tormented.

Reverend Peters had recently been begging me again to provide the special music at church. As was my typical response, I asked if he was desperate. As was *his* typical answer, he informed me that everyone always enjoyed it when I sang. When I ran out of excuses, I finally agreed. After all, in a small congregation, everyone had to do his or her part. I didn't like singing in public because my voice was deeper than most women's. I had a deep, soulful voice that seemed to overwhelm our small sanctuary. I also didn't like being the focus of everyone's attention, so I always felt self-conscious when I sang.

I was surprised to see Ellie sitting in the pew on the Sunday morning after our meeting. It had only been a few days since then, and I wondered what made her decide to come. She had made it clear that she did not attend church, and when we talked, she did not seem interested in attending any time soon.

When it was time for me to sing, I walked to the front of the church, nervous as always. I had selected an old hymn that my grandmother and I had both loved called "Wonderful Peace."

> *Far away in the depths of my spirit tonight*
> *Rolls a melody sweeter than psalm;*
> *In celestial-like strains it unceasingly falls*
> *O'er my soul like an infinite calm.*

And the refrain,

> *Peace, peace, wonderful peace,*
> *Coming down from the Father above!*
> *Sweep over my spirit forever, I pray*
> *In fathomless billows of love.*

> *I am resting tonight in the wonderful peace,*
> *Resting sweetly in Jesus control;*
> *For I'm kept from all danger by night and by day,*
> *And His glory is flooding my soul!*

> *Peace, peace, wonderful peace,*
> *Coming down from the Father above!*
> *Sweep over my spirit forever, I pray*
> *In fathomless billows of love.*

My favorite verse was the last one.

Ah soul, are you here without comfort and rest,
Marching down the rough pathway of time?
Make Jesus your friend ere the shadows grow dark;
Oh, accept this sweet peace so sublime!

Peace, peace, wonderful peace,
Coming down from the Father above!
Sweep over my spirit forever, I pray
In fathomless billows of love.

My soul had ached for years without comfort and rest because of my unaddressed trauma. It had taken a long time to find that wonderful peace, and I hoped the congregation realized I believed and lived this hymn. When I finished the song, I noticed a few ladies had retrieved handkerchiefs from their purses. Even Ellie didn't try to hide her emotions. She had tears streaming down her face. It appeared this hymn spoke to others as it did to me.

After the service, I stopped to visit with a few of my neighbors and fellow worshipers. We discussed the weather and how it would impact the planting season, and I inquired about one neighbor's recovery from a recent surgery. When I was done catching up with everyone, I noticed that Ellie was still in the sanctuary. She and Sam appeared to be having a serious conversation. She was drying her eyes with a tissue, and Sam was whispering in her ear. I wondered if I should interrupt, but I finally decided I should.

"Hello, Ellie. Hi, Sam. I hope I'm not intruding," I said as I approached them.

Sam answered, "Not at all, Lydia, but I'm sorry. I need to go."

I couldn't hide the surprise on my face as he walked away.

Ellie turned to me. "It's okay. I had just told Sam I wanted to talk to you."

"Okay. I was worried I had upset him. What's up?"

"If the invitation is still open, I would love to come over for coffee again."

"Of course. I would love that. When would you like to come?"

"If it works for you, tomorrow would be great."

"I don't have any plans at all tomorrow, so that would be wonderful."

After we finished lunch and cleaned the kitchen, I told Aunt Lu that I needed to clear my mind. I knew I should spend time preparing for a meeting with one of my clients, but I couldn't focus. It was a bit of a paradox, but my long hikes could both clear my mind and provide me with answers for my life's ponderings and with ideas concerning my clients. Since I had moved back home, hiking had become one of my favorite activities. When I first moved back, I realized that I was a workaholic and that tendency occasionally crept back into my new life. When I wasn't actively working to establish my own firm, I was thinking about it. I took up hiking not only for health reasons but also to force myself to take a work break. I quickly learned that I enjoyed this new activity, and I especially loved going to Gentry Woods. I loved the fresh air, the beauty of nature, and even the exercise. Because I left the distractions of technology behind, I was also able to relax and focus on enjoying the moment. And no distractions also meant it was easier to hear God's quiet voice.

Gentry Woods was a local treasure. Surrounded by acres of farm fields, it contained nearly a thousand acres of native forests and an abundance of wildflowers. It was a place of beauty in any season, and every new season, I felt *that* one was the prettiest. From the open and clear view in winter when there were no leaves to hide the birds and animals that stayed all year, to the first flowers in the spring, to the cool breeze felt under the canopy of trees in the summer, and to the amazing colors of fall—this place was nature at its best, and I was thankful someone had the foresight to set aside this land and protect it. As I took the three-mile loop through the property, I was thrilled to see that the bluebells were just beginning to bloom. They were one of my favorites!

I walked and prayed and thought. My coffee date loomed over me. I wondered about what might have changed for Ellie and about why she wanted to meet again so soon. The panic in her voice told me there was something wrong. My brain then raced from Ellie to one of my clients. He wanted to set up a trust, and I wasn't sure the best way to proceed to meet his needs.

As I enjoyed the scenery around me, I suddenly thought of some colleagues I could consult for advice on the trust. That simple plan eased my mind, and I stopped to take a deep breath. I was glad I did because I was blessed to discover the trillium was also blooming. I hadn't come up with any new answers about Ellie, but this hike had been just what my body and my soul needed. I drove back home with renewed peace.

Chapter 5

ELLIE ARRIVED RIGHT ON SCHEDULE. Aunt Lu had decided to run errands, so we had the house to ourselves for our conversation. After pouring coffee, we sat down at the kitchen table. Ellie stared into her cup. I waited for her to say something while the clock ticked away the minutes, but then I finally decided it was time for me to start the conversation.

"Something seems to be on your mind today," I said gently.

"Yes."

Silence. I waited again, and then I finally asked, "Do you want to talk about it?"

"It seems odd to share this with you, Lydia. We don't know each other that well. It's not like we were friends in school. And yet, well, it feels like I'm supposed to talk to you about this."

"Take your time. Share whatever and whenever it feels right."

"The song you sang at church yesterday about peace—it hit me. I don't remember when I last felt any peace in my life."

There was another extended period of silence.

"Why do you think that is?" I asked, prodding her to continue.

Tears appeared in Ellie's eyes, but she tried to dry them before I could notice. It was a move I had mastered earlier in my life when I was adamant about never showing any emotion. I knew instinctively it would be unwise to rush this conversation. If I pushed too quickly, she would leave and never share what she seemed desperate to tell me.

Finally, Ellie took a deep breath and began to tell me her story.

"My husband is unfaithful and abusive. I mean, he doesn't hit me, but I think it might be less painful if he did. He's cruel, and he puts me down every chance he can. He even compares me to his mistresses. He tells me they are prettier than me, how their bodies are better, and he even tells me details about their lovemaking. His only goal seems to be to cause me pain. He loves it on the rare occasion when I cry. I've worked hard to be able to hear anything he says and not show emotion, but the stronger I act, the worse his stories become."

I was outraged. I thought he had been an arrogant jerk in high school, but this was worse than I imagined.

"Why don't you leave him, Ellie?"

"And go where? And do what? He's made sure I don't have any job skills. I worked to put him through college when we were first married, but once he graduated, he demanded that I never have a job so he could completely control me. And you know his family. They are big-shot businesspeople in this town, owning their own businesses. Everyone looks up to them, or at least up to their money." She paused and tears formed in her eyes again. "My deepest fear is that if I left him . . . I'm afraid he would make sure that I would never see our daughter again."

That was the final straw for her. She put her head on the table and sobbed. I understood that emotional place—where you feel trapped with no options. My heart broke for her. I moved my chair to be closer and wrapped my arm around her shoulders. There was nothing to say, so I just sat with her in this place of pain and prayed.

When her crying subsided, she lifted her head, looked directly into my eyes, and asked, "Why am I not enough for him?"

Her question hit me hard. I squeezed her shoulders and said the only thing I could think of: "I don't have answers, Ellie, but I will sit here with you."

We sat quietly as our coffee became cold. Occasionally, I would see tears well up in her eyes again, but her years of controlling her emotions seemed to make them evaporate before they could fall. I wanted to talk to her about the problem of pushing down emotions and to share all the lessons I had learned the hard way, but I knew that needed to wait. Today was about listening and simply sitting with her in her pain.

Ellie found a tissue in her purse, blew her nose, and told me she needed to go. If she didn't have lunch on the table at noon, her husband would be furious. He went home almost every day for lunch and expected her to serve him.

As we said goodbye, I shared my parting thoughts. "I don't have any answers today, Ellie," I repeated. "But I would like to give some thought to what you could do. You should not have to continue to live like this. You have options."

She considered what I said and nodded. "All I ask is you keep this to yourself. I don't want him to know I've told you anything. And I don't want Sam to know either. I'm not sure how he would react."

"You have my word."

Sam's intuition about his sister amazed me. He knew something was wrong, but she wouldn't talk to him about it. I'm sure Ellie was afraid Sam would confront her husband, and that would make life more difficult for her. I had lost a little sleep before Ellie and I met for coffee, wondering what she wanted to talk about, but now I could not get her off my mind.

As I thought about Ellie throughout the next day, I kept thinking that I needed to talk to Gail. I wasn't sure what advice she would have, but Ellie's stories brought back memories of my past traumas. Those memories still caused me to lose my balance mentally and emotionally, and I thought talking to Gail would help me as I processed what I was feeling. As soon as I thought she would be home from school that afternoon, I called her.

"Hi, Gail."

"Hello, friend."

"Do you have time for a serious chat?" I asked.

"Oh, that sounds ominous, but yes, I do."

Without mentioning any names or identifying details, I told Gail what was going on.

"Oh, Lydia, this is so awful," she said when I was finished.

"I know, and I'm not sure what to do," I explained. "I'm not a therapist, and I'm not sure that my legal experience is what she needs at this point."

Gail was quiet for a moment, seemingly thinking. Then she said, "I think we need to start with step one."

"Which is?"

"Take a deep breath and pray. Also, there is no way you can help this person completely by yourself. You are going to need to include some others. Taking a deep breath will help clear your mind, and you know the power of prayer as well as I do. I think you will have some more wisdom after taking that first step."

"You're right," I said. "I resorted right back to my old habits of trying to fix everything by myself."

"Old habits come back quickly when we are under pressure. That's another reason to take a deep breath and pray. I will also ask our school social worker if she knows any agencies you could reach out to."

"That would be wonderful, Gail. I appreciate it. And now I'm going to let you go so I can pray about this. For some reason, I think I need to work quickly on some options."

As soon as I hung up the phone, I prayed for Ellie, and I prayed for guidance about how to help her. I also prayed for God's help in setting aside the memories of my own past trauma so that I could focus on Ellie's situation. It occurred to me that I needed to schedule another appointment with my therapist very soon. Friends, faith, and journaling had helped me immensely in my healing, but talking to a professional had been life-changing.

My grandmother had been the one who encouraged me to seek professional help. She encouraged me through one of the lessons she had written for me in a journal she titled "Lessons for Lydia." It was a book of lessons that she wanted to share with me in person, but she couldn't because I had closed myself off from my past and my family. Her words of wisdom had been tremendously helpful and comforting on my road to healing. They also helped me realize what a wise woman Grandmother was. Grandmother had been a teacher, and it was no surprise to me that she found a way to continue teaching even after her death. I wished we could have discussed these lessons together, but I knew

I had not been ready to hear them and learn from them earlier. Some learning cannot be rushed.

I decided to pull out her journal and reread a lesson.

My dearest Lydia,

I have always considered myself a lifelong learner. Any day that I can learn something new is a good and productive day. I have recently been reading about mental health. My focus has not been on a specific topic, but instead has been a broad overview of current research and thoughts. My dear child, I've known for years that there is a deep pain within you—something awful that you've hidden from and pushed down deep inside you. I don't know the cause, but I've seen the results of the pain.

I apologize for the disservice I did you by not pursuing more help when you were a teenager. It is no excuse, but my generation looked at counseling with a raised eyebrow. We thought everyone should pull themselves up by their proverbial bootstraps and solve problems on their own. I didn't think counseling was the answer. I was wrong to think that way, and I am sorry.

I've learned a bit about trauma and other situations that could have been impacting you and about how a therapist might have been helpful to you. In fact, my reading has shown me that almost everyone could benefit from therapy. We often need another person to help us process our struggles and discover solutions. We need someone who can pose the questions we need to ask ourselves and then help us to know if we have dug deep enough to find the answers. If you have not sought professional help to assist you with overcoming your pain, I urge you to consider taking this step. Life is too short to live with the pain I have seen you carry all your life.

You also need to know there is no shame in seeking help. It is not a character flaw to admit something is not right. I also want you to hear this—it often takes strength and courage to ask for help, and you are a strong and courageous woman. Please take this step for yourself. You deserve it.

I remembered back to when I had first read that lesson. I had found such encouragement from her words, that I closed the book and immediately made a few calls to find a therapist. I was blessed to find one, and I had appreciated her thoughtful questions ever since.

The school social worker was the first answer to my prayers for Ellie. After our call, Gail had talked to her the next day before school began, and the social worker called me immediately. She provided me with the name and contact information for an organization she had previously worked with that assisted women who experienced domestic violence or sexual assault. I immediately called them and spoke to one of the therapists on their staff.

I had a difficult time hearing all of this information. One concerning point I learned was that abuse often escalates, and the escalation often occurs when the abused spouse seeks help. When

I was listening to my therapist explain escalation in an abusive situation, I felt myself beginning to hyperventilate. Memories and emotions of my own rape came rushing back to me. I forced myself to tell my therapist that I needed a moment to take a deep breath and compose myself. She was not surprised by my response, and she shared that, often, people had no idea about the seriousness of the problem when abuse was involved. I explained that my friend's abuse was verbal and mental. The therapist told me that these types of abuse can suddenly escalate to physical violence.

We also discussed housing options and available career services. Ellie's situation was not unique in her having limited job skills. I learned that it is a common tool of abusers to make sure their spouses are dependent on them and have few options. A lack of options means many abused women feel that they have no choice but to stay with their abusers. Ellie was also not alone in worrying about what would happen to her daughter. It is common for domestic abuse survivors to believe they will lose in a battle over who can better financially provide for the children.

When I hung up the phone with the therapist, I told Aunt Lu I was going outside for a while. I needed fresh air, but I didn't feel like taking a walk, so I curled up in a chair on the porch. The intensity of the anxiety I felt surprised me. I gently told myself that I understood what I was feeling and the fear that had moved in, but I needed to focus on Ellie right now. I also reminded myself that I was safe, but I wasn't sure that Ellie was. My breathing returned to normal. My emotions would need to be addressed, but I was calmer now and could focus on Ellie's situation instead.

One point kept coming back to me: Ellie needed to get out of that house. I knew I needed to call Ellie soon and ask to meet with her again. We would face this next step together and make a plan. My growing list of resources could help with whatever that would be. I knew Sam would also be willing to help, but I could not talk to him until I had Ellie's permission. Although she was not technically my client, I felt I had a duty to hold what she had told me in confidence. Besides, I had given her my word.

Reflecting on everything I had learned, I decided that I would call Ellie in the morning, immediately after her daughter left on the bus for school.

Chapter 6

A SURPRISE VISITOR later that evening alerted me to the fact that I would not need to call Ellie in the morning after all. When I answered a knock at the door, I was surprised to find Ellie and her daughter, Jordyn, standing there. They each wore a different expression, but they shared a raw woundedness in both sets of eyes. Alarmed at their unannounced visit, I immediately invited them in. Aunt Lu heard their voices and wandered into the room, but when she saw their pained expressions, I think she could tell that something horrible had happened. She then did what Aunt Lu always did.

"Jordyn, dear, you look like you could use something to eat," she said, smiling at Ellie's daughter. "I baked one of my favorite cookies today. Would you be willing to have some with me? Cookies always taste better when you share them with others." Jordyn's expression brightened at the mention of dessert, and after her mother nodded her approval, she hurried away with Aunt Lu, leaving Ellie and me alone in the doorway.

I suggested that we go to the living room. Ellie said nothing but followed me into the room, where she collapsed into a chair. I thought she was going to start crying, but then I remembered she was in shock, and the tears she desperately needed to shed likely would not come. Her body was in protection mode.

"Do you want to talk about it?" I asked.

"He snapped and I woke up. He threatened me in front of Jordyn. I finally realized his abuse could escalate from mental and emotional to physical. There is no way I want her to think this is what a healthy marriage looks like. I can't have her witnessing this messed-up marriage. And I can't risk our physical safety.

"I'm so sorry we just showed up on your doorstep. I didn't know what else to do. When Clark went to the bathroom, I grabbed Jordyn's arm and my purse, and we jumped in my car."

"Ellie, I'm so glad you came here. I know this is hard, but we are going to face this together."

"I thought about going to Sam's, but I'm so afraid of how he would react. I know he's suspected something was wrong for a long time. When we're together, he just looks at me in the way that he does. He has a way of seeing into your soul. I was afraid he might do something we would all regret."

Coming to my house was probably the hardest thing she had ever done.

"I understand," I told her. "You've taken the first step by leaving. Why don't you stay here tonight, and we can decide step two tomorrow?" I was prepared to insist on her staying at the farmhouse if I needed to, but thankfully, Ellie agreed. The pained look on her face told the story, and we both knew she needed to try and rest before deciding what to do next.

Aunt Lu and I quickly tidied Grandmother's room for Ellie and Jordyn. We would figure out ongoing arrangements later, but this seemed like the best option for the first night. Neither one said much, so after Grandmother's room was ready, we left them to get settled, and I headed back down to the living room to sit and try to compose myself.

I had barely taken a breath when I heard the unmistakable

sound of tires on the gravel driveway, and those tires were moving fast. *Who could it be now?* I wondered as I jumped out of my chair and ran to the door. I peeked out the door's window just in time to watch Ellie's husband, Clark, jump out of his truck. My heart started pounding as I ducked down from the glass. I had hoped we would have until tomorrow before we had to face him.

He was obviously eager to have a confrontation as soon as possible, because he raced up the sidewalk, took the stairs two at a time, and started banging on the door.

"Where's my wife?" he shouted.

I slowly opened the door.

"Hello, Clark," I said. "Can I help you?"

He ignored me and continued his rant. "Don't tell me she's not here! When I didn't see her car at Sam's place, I remembered the day she told me that lunch was late because she'd been over here drinking coffee! Then it all hit me: she's been spending time with you, and you've filled her head with garbage. You think you're all high and mighty with your big legal career. I'm sure you've told her she would be better off without me. I demand to see her!"

I'm not an imposing or particularly strong woman, but I was determined he was not entering my home. I had faced abusers and bullies before, and I was determined this was one battle I was going to win. I quickly moved to completely block the door.

"You are not seeing your wife this evening."

"How dare you! Move out of my way or I'm knocking you out of my way." He took a step toward me, but I resisted the urge to back away. He was close enough now that I would easily be in his grasp. I kept a tight grip on the door handle partly to steady myself and partly to ensure he didn't push it open to go around me.

In a calm voice that could only have been sent by God, I said,

"Clark, you are not going to see your wife tonight. This is your only warning. If you do not get back in your truck and leave my property, I will have Aunt Lu call the police and every neighbor as well." And then I stared at him. I didn't move, and I didn't break eye contact.

Every muscle in his body tensed up. I wondered if he was going to hit me or shove me out of his way. Time slowed down. It seemed that we stared at each other for hours, but I'm sure it was less than a minute.

At last, in a voice filled with barely controlled rage, he said, "Fine. But this isn't over, Lydia. Not even close. You were a nothing in high school, and you are a nothing now. I don't know what garbage you've filled my wife's head with, but this isn't over." He punctuated those last three words as if each one was a sentence of its own.

He stomped his way off the porch and down the sidewalk, jerked open the truck door, and slammed it closed again after he climbed in. Then he sped out in his truck, throwing gravel into the air behind him. I waited until I couldn't hear his vehicle anymore before I breathed a sigh of relief.

Aunt Lu came up behind me and placed her hand on my shoulder. "Oh, Lydia, I don't know where your bravery came from."

I nodded, but my heart had not slowed down enough for me to say anything.

We were still standing at the door when I heard another vehicle flying down the long driveway. I tensed again. Was Clark already back for another round? My mind had begun to race with worries about what to say or how to keep ourselves safe, when I caught a glimpse of the truck racing toward the house. It was Sam.

"Sam?" I said aloud. "How did—"

"I didn't call the police, but I did call Sam," Aunt Lu said, interrupting me.

The truck skidded to a stop, and Sam climbed out of it almost before it had stopped moving.

"Where's Clark?" he said, rushing to the doorway.

Aunt Lu could tell I was still a little dazed by the encounter, so she jumped in. "Sam, you should have seen Lydia. She blocked the door and told Clark he wasn't seeing Ellie tonight. I couldn't see her face, but I could see Clark's. I think he was a little scared of her. I'll say I've never heard her use that tone before. But we sure are glad you are here."

"Yes, Sam, we are. Come in. I think we need to talk."

Sam stepped into the house, and I closed and locked the door behind him. When I turned back to the room, I was surprised to find Ellie standing at the bottom of the stairs, tears streaming down her face.

"Lydia, Lu, I'm so sorry to involve you in this. And Sam, I'm so sorry I didn't tell you anything earlier, but I was afraid of how you would react."

Aunt Lu nodded to Ellie and excused herself to go to bed and get some sleep, but I doubted any of us would be able to rest.

"Ellie, would you like me to leave while you two talk?" I asked after Aunt Lu had gone to her room.

"No, please stay, Lydia. Your presence is calming to me. I made sure Jordyn was asleep before I came down because I don't want her to overhear this conversation."

Her comment surprised me, but I agreed to stay to support her as she told Sam her story. We settled into comfortable seats in the living room as Ellie shared the details. When she finished,

Sam looked at the floor and said, "I want to kill him, but I know that's not God's way."

I spoke for the first time since Ellie had started her story. "Sam, you're obviously right. That is not God's way. But it also isn't God's desire for Ellie to be treated as she has been. Even though Jesus told us to turn the other cheek, he did not intend for women to live in fear of their husbands or to be abused like this. That's not what Jesus meant, and it's not how he wants us to live."

I turned my attention to Ellie. "You will have to make decisions about how you want to move forward. I'm here to help you any way I can, and I know Sam is too."

Sam nodded and added, "Anything you need."

Then I added, "Long-term decisions don't have to be made tonight, but I suppose how you want to handle tomorrow does need to be decided."

"I think the only decision I can make tonight is that when Clark comes back, I will talk to him. And I will tell him Jordyn and I are moving out. Beyond that, I don't know. I don't think I can decide anything else tonight."

"I think that's enough decision making for tonight," I reassured her.

After a long night of talking, Ellie and I went upstairs to get some sleep. Sam said he would sleep on the couch in case Clark came back.

After only a couple hours of sleep, before the sun could even rise, I got out of bed. Intuition told me that Clark would be back any minute. I crept quietly down to the kitchen, started the coffee maker, and set the table for breakfast. Sam heard me, and he shuffled into the kitchen.

"Is the coffee ready?" he asked.

"Almost. Did you get any sleep?"

"Not much. How about you?"

"Same as you," I answered.

"I'm still extremely angry, but I've decided I will handle this like any other problem: with prayer and by remaining levelheaded."

I smiled. "You amaze me, Sam. I'm not sure I would respond that way if the roles were reversed. I admire your faith."

"I realized Clark's not worth going to prison over. But he better not push me."

I poured two mugs of strong coffee, and we sat down to drink them and eat some apple-bran muffins. It wasn't long before both Aunt Lu and Ellie joined us. Ellie looked terrible. Aunt Lu apparently agreed with me because she asked her if she should go back to bed.

"Thank you, Lu, but I figure Clark will be here soon, and I need some coffee first."

As if on cue, we heard a truck pull into the drive. Sam's expression grew dark. I set my mug on the table, stood, and forced myself to walk calmly to the front door just as Clark stormed up the steps. I greeted him in a calm-but-no-nonsense voice.

"Good morning, Clark," I said.

Again he ignored me and got right to the point. "Now, Lydia, I left last night, but I demand to see my wife this morning."

"You may see her with the following conditions. First, you will keep your voice down because your daughter is still sleeping. And second, you will treat Ellie with respect."

"Fine. But you and Sam stay out of my way. I saw his truck, so I know he's here."

I sighed. "I guess I need to add another condition. Third, Sam and I will stay out of the living room, but we will stand by so that all Ellie needs to do is say the word and we will join you."

I looked him straight in the eyes again and didn't back down. Clark finally lowered his gaze, sighed, and muttered, "Fine."

Sam and I stood at the kitchen doorway so we could hear if Ellie called for us. I could not hear every word of their conversation, but I did hear Clark begging Ellie to forgive him. He voiced the classic line of abusers, "I will change, I promise."

One of the domestic violence counselors I had spoken to told me that most abusers would beg forgiveness and act loving, but it wouldn't take long for the hostile words and actions to begin again. I learned that abusers rarely intend to change because they don't believe they are part of the problem. Instead, it is part of their tactic, either consciously or subconsciously, to keep their victims in their grip.

Although I couldn't hear every word of the conversation, I could tell that Clark's tone was becoming increasingly hostile. Eventually, I heard him call Ellie every name in the book, and then he moved on to Sam and me as well. I didn't hear what he said about Sam, but I clearly heard what he said about me. He told Ellie that if she wanted to move in with the school tramp, she could stay where she was. He then threatened to make sure she never saw her daughter again because he would prove I was a negative influence on everyone around me.

Ellie's response was very audible. "Our daughter will not be a pawn in the problems that are between you and me." I wanted to cheer for her, but I remained quiet. After all, this was heartbreaking. I was certain I was witnessing the end of a marriage. I was also concerned about Clark's comment about me. I prayed that Sam didn't hear him or didn't pay attention to it since Clark was making wild accusations about all of us. It was an upsetting scene for everyone involved.

Finally, Clark stormed out of the house without saying a word to Sam or me. We went into the living room to be with Ellie. She was sitting on the sofa looking out the window with a stoic look on her face. I went and knelt beside her and put my hand on her knee. That simple act of kindness caused her to start sobbing. She spoke no words, but all her emotions came rolling out in wave after wave of tears. I sat quietly because I knew from experience that words were not always necessary. God was with us, and God would provide the comfort Ellie was able to receive at this moment.

When she had no tears left, Ellie looked up at me and then at Sam and said, "I'm so sorry."

"There is absolutely nothing for you to be sorry about," I responded.

"Lydia's right. It's that loser who needs to be sorry," Sam said.

I shot Sam a look that warned him to stop.

He took a breath and then added, "I'm sorry, Ellie. I know he's still your husband, but he hurt you, and that makes me furious."

"I know, Sam. I know." She was quiet for a moment and then said, "I need to check on Jordyn."

Since it was still quite early, we weren't surprised when she came back downstairs and told us Jordyn was still asleep. After a long discussion, it was decided that Ellie and Jordyn would move in with Sam. My house was bigger, but Sam said he would never sleep again unless they were with him, so it was agreed.

We decided we would all go to Ellie's and pack up what they needed. We planned to wait until the time when Clark typically left for work. I prayed he would follow his normal schedule and be gone by the time we arrived.

Chapter 7

IT DIDN'T TAKE LONG for Ellie and Jordyn to settle into Sam's house. The next order of business was for Ellie to find a job. She knew it was unlikely that she would find a job that paid very well, but at this point anything would be helpful. Thankfully, her expenses were low since she was living with her brother. A kindhearted businessperson decided to take a chance on her and hired her to be his administrative assistant. Ellie was thrilled to embark on a career less than a month after leaving her husband. She was especially excited to know that after she became acclimated to the job, she would eventually take over some of the bookkeeping duties of the business. I don't think I'd ever met someone who was so thankful for the smallest act of kindness. It made me realize how little kindness she had likely experienced over the last few years.

Rather than stay home alone, Jordyn was supposed to spend time with Sam when she wasn't in school. Not long after Ellie started her job, Sam and Jordyn came over to visit. Sam had bribed her with the promise of some of Aunt Lu's fabulous baked goods. Even though it wasn't early for me, it must have been an early morning for Jordyn because she looked like she had just rolled out of bed.

"Jordyn, you look a little sleepy. Would you like a cup of

coffee to go with your pecan roll? A big coffee is the only thing that wakes me up in the morning," I said.

"Lydia, she's still a kid. She doesn't drink coffee," Sam told me.

"Oh, a little coffee never hurt anybody." I winked at Jordyn.

"I'm not sure I would like it, but could I try some?" she asked.

Sam nodded that it was okay, and I grabbed another mug from the cabinet and poured her a steaming cup.

"I'm always looking for someone new to introduce to coffee. I suppose it is a selfish act on my part because then I have another person to enjoy coffee and conversation with," I said, handing her the mug.

Jordyn took a sip and almost spit it out. She tried to pretend to like it and thus perhaps be closer to being an adult, but it was obvious that she didn't like it.

"I should have offered some creamer to go in your coffee. It will add a bit of sweetness and cut the bitter flavor. Would you like some?"

"I guess so," she answered.

I poured some into her cup. It was more than I would use for myself, but not as much as others use. Some people seem to add a little coffee to their cup of creamer. "What do you think now?" I asked.

Jordyn took a tentative sip. "The creamer helped."

Sam piped in, "Coffee is an acquired taste. I didn't like it at all when I first tried it."

"Then why did you keep drinking it?" she asked.

"Like Lydia said, I needed something to help me wake up."

Jordyn nodded her understanding but didn't say much else.

As Sam and Jordyn were finishing up their pecan rolls, I had an idea. I said, "Jordyn, I'm getting ready to go for a hike. Would you like to join me? I'm going to the creek. It's a good workout, and the scenery is pretty."

Jordyn's facial expressions were as stoic as they come, so I wasn't sure what she was thinking. After sitting for a minute, she agreed. She said it would be better than riding around with her uncle all day. I told Sam we would find him later. Or, if we were having a great time, he could come back to the house and pick her up. We finished our coffee, said our goodbyes, and then headed outside.

As we walked, I tried to get Jordyn to open up to me a bit. I asked her questions about her classes and her friends. All I received were one-word, barely audible answers. Since I had little experience with teenagers, I wasn't sure what else to do or what else to ask. I decided to share a bit about my own teen years to see if that would break the ice.

"You know, I didn't enjoy my teen years. I wasn't cool, and I wasn't sure I wanted to be anyway. I was also shy, and I didn't have many friends. To be honest, I'm not sure I had any real friends. Life was a challenge for me back then, and I was glad when I graduated and could leave. So, I surprised myself when I decided to move back here."

Jordyn stopped and looked at me. "I thought these were supposed to be the best years of my life. No responsibilities and all the fun are what I've been told."

I shook my head. "I'm going to disagree with what you've been told," I said. "Those years were certainly not the best for me. And I think you do have some responsibilities. Fewer than what you will have when you're an adult, but you don't have the same privileges as an adult right now, either."

Jordyn nodded her agreement. Maybe I was reaching her. I didn't know, but I was hoping I was.

When we reached the creek, I pointed out some animal prints in the mud. We speculated on what might have made the tracks. I also pointed out some lovely wildflowers. Jordyn continued with her one-word answers and her disinterested expressions.

On our way back to the house, I decided to continue making conversation by asking more questions.

"Your uncle told me you are a good athlete. What's your favorite sport?"

Jordyn rolled her eyes. "Everybody says I'm a good athlete. Dad insisted I be named Jordyn because he loved Michael Jordan. So, of course he thinks I'm supposed to be some star athlete."

She caught me off guard with her reaction. I had obviously hit a nerve, and I wasn't sure how to respond. We kept walking as I thought about what to say next. I finally said, "Okay, I gather that you don't care for sports even though you play them. What other activities do you enjoy more?"

"You're not going to tell my dad, are you?" she asked.

"No. That's not my story to tell."

"Good. I don't want to cause problems right now."

"I understand."

She thought for a moment before responding. "I like music. I like band and chorus. I even got a part in the school musical."

"That's wonderful, Jordyn!"

"Yeah, well, my dad says it's taking time and energy away from sports. He says he won't come watch because musicals are dumb."

I had to take a deep breath. I had never liked this guy in high school, and I'd learned the years had not changed my opinion. But this was her father, so I refused to say anything negative. Instead, I said, "I would love to come see you in the musical."

"Really?"

"Yes, really. I love musicals. Always have."

"That would be great! And then my mom would have someone to sit with."

We walked back to the house in silence. I didn't know what Jordyn was thinking, but I was praying. I prayed for the right words to help this young person. And I prayed for patience so that I could deal with her father without making anything worse.

Chapter 8

I HAD BEEN SO FOCUSED on a work project and tasks around the house that I had found no time to enjoy being outside. As I thought about it, I wasn't sure why those projects and tasks had occupied so much time, but I knew it had been two or perhaps even three weeks since I had spent any significant amount of time basking in nature. When I realized it was a beautiful spring day, I decided to go outside and enjoy it. I had grown to cherish spending time outside. The immense size and the diversity of God's wonderful creation filled my soul. I always felt peace when I strolled around this beautiful farm.

My first destination was the apple orchard. After spending time enjoying the trees, I decided to stroll through and admire the numerous flower beds my grandparents had created long ago. As I walked, I breathed in deeply and exhaled slowly, allowing nature to fill me. The flower beds always filled me with such joy. Grandmother loved growing many different types of flowers in a wide variety of colors. At this time of year, the beds of tulips, daffodils, and hyacinths were especially beautiful. Like Grandmother, I loved the variety of colors, and I also loved how each flower bloomed in its own time. Flowers didn't compare themselves to other flowers, not in their appearance nor in their timing. They were content in the rhythm of God's design. They always bloomed at just the right moment for them.

Today was also a perfect day to spend time at the creek, so I walked there next. There hadn't been a path when I first began going to the creek, but through my frequent visits, I made my own. There was something calming about the water flowing over the rocks. The creek was almost dry during the late summer when rain was infrequent, and I always missed that sound. But now, the spring rains meant the water was quite high. It rushed over the rocks like mini white-water rapids. On this trip, I noticed there were even more animal tracks near the water than when Jordyn and I had made the trek. I was fascinated by these tracks, but I wasn't very good at identifying the animals that made them.

When I took these walks, it was my practice to pray. Today, I thanked God for all this glorious creation, for the colors, and the diversity of plants and animals. I then prayed for everyone I knew who was hurting. Ellie was at the top of this list. The pain I'd felt in my past relationships helped me to empathize with her. We had each been deeply wounded by people, and I asked God to help heal her.

Jordyn was next on my mind. She seemed to be emotionally shut down. The vacant look in her eyes reminded me of myself. For years, I had been convinced that showing emotions would somehow reveal all my pain to others. As a defense, I built walls around myself so people could not see who I really was. It had taken time and significant work to tear those walls down and to begin allowing people in. I hoped I could help Jordyn do the same, but I wasn't sure if she was ready or if she would even allow me to help her. Regardless, somehow I needed to let her know she wasn't alone. God would be with her during this difficult and painful time, and I would also be there for her. She needed supporters in her corner, and I hoped I could be one of those for her.

It was hard to believe so much time had already passed since I'd spent time with Jordyn. It felt like it had only been a few days, but in reality, it had been almost a month. When I had recently seen Ellie at church, she mentioned that Jordyn had been very busy with rehearsals for the school musical and with trying to keep up with her homework. It sounded as if she barely had time to sleep. I told Ellie that Jordyn and I had taken a walk and that I had enjoyed our time together. She had smiled and said that was probably the last nonstructured activity she'd had before her life became so busy.

I could tell from Ellie's comments that Jordyn was living in survival mode, trying to get through her busy schedule of musical rehearsals and homework. There was no need to ask how she was handling her parents' separation or how she was feeling about anything else at the moment. She had been keeping herself too busy to think about or process what was happening in her family life. I made a mental note to spend some time with her after the musical, which was scheduled to happen in a few days.

After finishing my prayers, I glanced at my watch and realized how long I had been gone. I didn't want Aunt Lu to worry, so I decided to get back to the house. Besides, I knew there was some work on my to do list for the day.

When I returned from my walk, Aunt Lu told me Gail had called while I was out. I decided to return her call before I looked at my to do list. She answered my call on the first ring.

"Wow, that was fast. Did your phone even ring?"

"Hey, Lydia. I've been making a few phone calls, and I had

just finished talking to someone. So, your timing is perfect. Guess what time of year it is?" she asked.

"Well, it's spring, but I'm not sure that's the answer you're looking for."

She laughed. "No, it's not the answer I'm looking for. I am very behind this year, but the answer I'm looking for is that it's time for me to teach the US constitution."

"Ah. Now I know what you're going to ask."

"And what will your answer be?"

"Do you honestly want me to come back and speak?"

"Yes, I do. You were a rock star last year, and the kids loved it."

"I don't know about rock-star status, but if you think the kids learned something, then sign me up. I think I saved my notes from last time."

"Thank you, Lydia. I appreciate it," she said. Then her tone grew a little more serious. "I also have another topic on my mind, if you have a minute."

"Sure. What's up?"

"I've been thinking we should start a women's book study or small group at church. I think several women would be interested."

"That does sound like a good idea."

"So, would you be willing to co-lead with me? I'm not sure I have time to tackle it on my own, but I thought we could share the duties."

"Geez, you are full of ideas to keep me busy! Weren't you telling me recently that my plate was overflowing? And that I seemed tired?" I joked.

Gail paused. "Yes, but I was thinking that you were working too hard at trying to start a business and that you were spending time on activities that drained you. I think this will, as they say, fill you up instead."

"Okay, I think I understand what you're saying. I've never led—or, rather, co-led—anything like this, but I'm willing to give it a try. Do we need to talk to Reverend Peters first?"

"I already have. I was talking to him about wanting a deeper sense of community, and he suggested forming some type of women's group. Although the material we study will be important, for me, the bigger goal is getting to know people better. It's about building a community of people to pray with and talk to."

I understood exactly what Gail was saying. Since I'd moved back to the farm, I'd wanted to develop friendships, but I had not been very successful. So far, Gail was the only person I had truly connected with. "I think that sounds like a wonderful idea. You may recall that my grandmother told me on countless occasions that I needed to be in a community of believers to support me. We can't do life alone."

"Amen!"

"Count me in," I told her.

"Wonderful. I think all we need is a meeting date, and then we can talk to women after church on Sunday to invite them. Maybe we could even make some invitations they can take home so they put it on their calendars."

"Great idea. That sounds like something I can handle, so I will get to work on that."

We ended our call, and I immediately went to work on creating some invitations. I had a good feeling about Gail's idea, and I was excited to begin.

Chapter 9

THE DAY OF JORDYN'S MUSICAL finally arrived! I couldn't explain why, but I was excited to see it and watch Jordyn do something I knew she was passionate about. It occurred to me that I had never asked what musical they were performing or what role she had. I was so irritated when she had told me her dad wouldn't go because he thought it was a waste of time, I lost focus on the details about the musical itself.

Ellie and I made plans to meet in the lobby at the school. She was waiting for me when I walked in, and my heart skipped as I saw a few young people in nun costumes. I realized they must be performing one of my favorite musicals, *The Sound of Music*. I couldn't contain my excitement.

"Ellie, I never thought to ask what musical I would see tonight, but I'm guessing by the costumes it must be *The Sound of Music*."

Ellie laughed and said, "You're so perceptive. Yes, that's the one."

"It's one of my absolute favorites. I love all of the songs. What role is Jordyn playing?"

"Liesl," she told me.

"Wow! That's an important role. Very impressive!"

"I had no idea she was so passionate about music. I think

she hid it from us because music is not what Clark wanted her to spend her time and energy on. He says it won't get her places."

"I think he's wrong. Pursuing our passions helps us become who we are meant to be. She may not become a professional musician, but music can bring her joy her entire life."

Ellie nodded. I didn't say anything else because I was afraid I would say something about Clark that I would regret.

We made our way to our seats, and soon, the lights dimmed around us. I found myself smiling as soon as the music began. Part of the reason I loved this musical was because my grandmother and I had watched it together. She loved the music as much as I did, and I felt so connected to her when I realized we shared a love for something. I remember watching the movie on TV as we sat on the couch together sharing a big bowl of popcorn. Grandmother didn't enjoy watching television, and this was one of the few times we watched TV together. She always said she much preferred reading a book.

As the musical continued, I found myself focusing almost exclusively on Jordyn. I was impressed by her confidence and poise on stage, and the tone and beauty of her voice were outstanding. The applause after the song "Sixteen Going on Seventeen" showed that I wasn't the only person who was impressed.

When the musical was over, the audience awarded the cast with a standing ovation. The kids had worked hard to put on such a splendid show, and everyone knew it. I looked over at Ellie and saw tears streaming down her face, so I put my arm around her shoulders.

"They all did a great job, but I had no idea Jordyn had such a beautiful voice."

"Honestly, I didn't either," Ellie replied. "I've never heard her sing around the house. I wish Clark would have come to support her, but he's never going to change."

I gave her shoulder a little squeeze. "You were here to support her, and that's what's important. I'm going to go tell her what a great job she did. Do you want to join me?"

Ellie wiped away her proud mom tears and nodded. In the lobby, the students in the cast stood in a line, greeting everyone as they left. Jordyn was glowing. Her passion for music was obvious. When she saw her mom, her smile grew even larger. Ellie's smile matched her daughter's, and she gave Jordyn a big hug when we approached and told her how proud she was of her.

"Thanks, Mom. I wish Dad would have come," Jordyn said.

"I know, honey. I know," Ellie told her.

"It's okay though. He would have just told me how bored he was."

"I know. He doesn't appreciate music like he does sports."

"I'm glad you were here."

"Me too, honey."

Ellie stepped aside, and then it was finally my turn to speak to her. Jordyn threw her arms around me.

"Thank you so much for coming!"

I gave her a tight hug in response and told her, "The joy was mine. You did a wonderful job in a very important role, and your voice is amazing. Promise me that you will continue to pursue this passion for as long and as far as you want."

She didn't say anything. She simply continued to beam that beautiful smile and then nodded. And on my drive home, I also continued to smile. I couldn't remember the last time I'd had an evening I enjoyed so much.

Chapter 10

Aunt Lu had been busy with one of her epic cooking sprees. She asked if I thought Sam, Ellie and Jordyn would like some meals. I told her I was certain they would love some. Ellie was still adjusting to the workflow of her new job, and one less task, such as cooking, would be a blessing. I gathered up all the food that Aunt Lu made and called Sam to make sure someone was home. He told me he was working on some equipment, but Jordyn was at the house. I hadn't talked to her since the night of the musical, so I thought I would tell her again how much I enjoyed it.

When I pulled in, Jordyn was kicking a soccer ball around the yard. I got out of my car and said, "I didn't think you liked playing sports. Why are you out here kicking a soccer ball?" I immediately regretted my words. "I'm so sorry Jordyn. That was rude. I was trying to put a label on you, and that wasn't fair."

She looked up at me and said, "I like being active. I just don't like people telling me what activities I have to do. And I don't like the pressure that comes with it. But I enjoy being outside after being stuck inside all day at school."

"Good for you. It's good to know what you like to do and to spend time outside getting some exercise. I also want to tell you again that I thought you were wonderful in the musical, and I thoroughly enjoyed it."

Jordyn smiled and blushed a little. "Thank you."

"Now, I'm wondering if you would mind helping me carry in all this food. Aunt Lu wanted to make sure you didn't go hungry! There are even some freshly baked chocolate chip cookies that might still be warm from the oven if we hurry," I told her. Jordyn quickly agreed to help. After we put the food away, I asked her if she thought it would be a good idea to take some of the cookies and two glasses of milk outside where we could enjoy the sun and our sweet treats. I was shocked when she smiled and said that sounded good!

Sam only had one folding chair outside, so we plopped onto the ground instead. After we finished our cookies and licked the melted chocolate from our fingers, we laid back on the grass. It felt almost decadent. My stomach was full of warm cookies and cold milk. Then to lay on the grass and feel the warmth of mother earth pour in through my skin all the way to my soul was heavenly. I felt somewhere between a child and a wise sage to be willing to do that and to be able to acknowledge the wisdom in that almost holy act. I let my body relax into the ground. I think it was the connection between my body and the earth that gave me courage.

"This is so nice to lie here like this. What are you feeling?" I asked.

"I don't know that I'm feeling anything," she said after a moment.

"Maybe you're feeling peaceful," I suggested.

"Yeah. Maybe."

I let the silence hang between us before saying, "I know it can be hard to find the words to describe how we feel sometimes."

"I guess. Sometimes I'm feeling so much I don't know what to say first."

"Yeah, I've been there too." I laid there, wondering if I should say anything else. I finally decided to jump in and share. "I've gone through some bad times when I thought my emotions were going to explode out of me."

Jordyn rolled on her side to look at me. "Really?"

"Oh yeah. I didn't know which of my emotions would come out first. I felt like I had a war fighting inside of me to see which one would win."

"I thought adults had everything figured out," she said.

"No, we don't. But I'm not so old that I've forgotten what it was like to be your age either."

Jordyn actually laughed. It was the first time I had heard it, so I decided to keep going.

"My mom and dad died when I was young, and I lived with my grandparents. It was hard. I knew they loved me, but I missed my family. I felt like I lost my parents and my grandparents at the same time. You see, my grandparents had to step into the parental role, so they couldn't be the fun grandparents who spoiled their grandchild."

"That must have been hard for you," Jordyn said.

I nodded. "Unfortunately, that wasn't the only tough thing I had to face. I was also hurt by someone I cared about. Then, I went to a very dark place. I wouldn't let people into my life. I shut everybody out so I wouldn't be hurt again. It took me years to heal and to acknowledge that I was never truly alone. Even when I was trying to hide from God, He was always right there waiting for me to reach out."

Jordyn rolled on her back again and looked up at the sky. "Well, I haven't been through anything like all of that."

"It's not a contest," I explained. "We each have our own pain that we carry. And I think you're going through something just as painful."

"You do?"

"Yes, I do. I don't know what it's like for you to watch your mom and dad go through such a hard time, but I'm guessing it hurts and that it's scary."

Jordyn laid there quietly. I was concerned I may have shared too much, so I decided to just wait and not be afraid of the silence. A person often needs time to process what they are thinking and feeling.

After what seemed like hours, Jordyn finally spoke again. "Lydia?"

"Yes?"

"I think their fighting is my fault."

I rolled on my side so I could see her. "Oh, honey, why do you think that?"

"I'm not good enough. I'm not a good enough student. I'm not a good enough athlete. I'm not a good enough daughter. If I were enough, they wouldn't fight about me and my activities. It's all my fault."

And then tears flooded her eyes. I asked if I could hug her, and she nodded as she sobbed. She cried the tears that had been locked away as she tried to be brave and strong.

Eventually her crying slowed, and she tried to catch her breath to talk.

"Please don't tell my mom and dad what I said."

"Oh, honey, I won't. But I do think you need to talk to your mom. I know she thinks you are enough, and I know she doesn't want you to hurt like this."

Jordyn sat up and rubbed her eyes. "I'll think about it."

"One other thing," I said. "The problems between parents are never a child's fault. It's between the adults. Please hear me on this."

"So, why then? Why are they getting divorced?"

"Are you sure that they are? I haven't heard that. But even if they do, I can't answer your question. Divorce is different for each couple. I just know it's not because of you."

She nodded and wiped away her tears. There was another long silence.

Eventually she said, "Lydia?"

"Yes?"

"Do you suppose it would be okay if we ate another cookie?"

I smiled. "I think another cookie sounds wonderful."

As I reflected on my conversation with Jordyn and on the memories of my past, I remembered another lesson Grandmother had written in her "Lessons for Lydia" journal. I pulled out the journal to reread the entry she wrote about the problems we face when we are focused on our past. Grandmother called it "Lot's Wife."

My child, you cannot fully step into your future while you are constantly looking over your shoulder at your past. Not only have I seen you looking back at your past; I've also seen you run and run, trying to move faster than your memories only to be stopped and forced to look at them again. When you try to run from the pain of your past instead of facing it, you will eventually discover that you are stuck there. Now, of course, you do need to learn lessons from the past—and there is nothing wrong with paying homage to your past and your traditions—but you cannot live there. You cannot grow and move forward if you are always worried about your problems and what's behind you.

The story of Lot's wife comes to mind. You may recall in Genesis 19 that, as their city was being destroyed, Lot and everyone with him were told not to stop and not to look back until they reached their destination. For some reason, Lot's wife turned back, and she was turned into a pillar of salt. Of course, I don't believe you will become a pillar of salt if you remain focused on your past. I do, however, believe that a person can become paralyzed when they spend more time looking backward, worrying about what happened yesterday instead of living in the moment. And when you are paralyzed by the past, your ability to move forward becomes difficult.

God wants you to put your trust in Him. God wants you to spend time in the present and not worry about the past. The past cannot be changed, so ask forgiveness for what needs to be forgiven and then leave the rest behind. Take the lessons learned with you but leave the guilt and shame behind.

When you dwell in your past, you cannot thoroughly receive the healing gifts of God's love and forgiveness that He wants for you. Remember this: what you focus on the most will be what defines you. It is time for a new start, Lydia. Dismiss the voices from the past and focus on the one that tell you of God's love for you. Live today with those new words guiding you, with your trust and faith in God.

This entry was even better than I remembered. I knew I couldn't focus on the past because it made it difficult to move into the future. And I loved that Grandmother talked about the voices we play in our mind. Those recordings often fill us with shame and guilt from the past and create anxiety about the future. It was good to be reminded that I needed to play new "tapes" in my mind, and what better one to play than one that tells me I am loved. I said a silent thank-you to Grandmother for blessing me with her wonderful wisdom once again.

Chapter 11

GAIL AND I STRUGGLED to find a book we thought a diverse group of women would enjoy. As we discussed the possibilities, we reminded ourselves that the book itself was not as important as the connections we would make. Our hope was that the group would become a community and that we would all grow to trust and rely on each other. So, we chose a book titled *It Is Well* and invited people to our first gathering the following week.

We were pleased that eight women from our small congregation attended our first meeting. I had invited Aunt Lu, but she declined as she had her own group that she enjoyed, and she thought I needed my own group. We began our first meeting by asking each woman to share not only her name, but something we might not know about her. Even in our small community, people didn't know each other as well as they thought. Then, we asked if anyone had a concern they wanted us to pray for or something they needed support for. The room was quiet. This was a room of stoic women, and I wondered if anyone would share anything.

A woman named Anna finally broke the ice and said she had something to share. "In a few short weeks, my husband and I will watch our baby graduate from high school. Then, in the fall, we will send this child to college. We've sent our three older children off to college already, but this feels different." She paused for a moment as she collected her thoughts. "Somehow the decades have flown by without me even noticing them. I don't understand how my baby is ready for college when I'm positive that I became a first-time mother just a few years ago."

"I agree with you that time seems to move faster the older we are," Ruth commented.

"I've always thought with all of our wonderful technology someone should be able to slow down the ticking clock so we can have longer to savor each minute," Rebecca added.

Kay responded, "That would make someone very rich! But honestly, you all look exactly the same as you have for years. I refuse to believe that any of you are aging."

I'm sure most of us took these comments lightly because we all knew there was no satisfactory way of slowing down the clock.

And then Anna voiced it—the big question—with a single tear running down her cheek. "But who will I be? How will I define myself without having children at home to raise?"

The feeling in the room changed immediately. One among us was hurting. This was not a casual groan about the passage of time. This was an SOS. Her question hit me hard, and I knew I would never forget it. *But who will I be?* She was asking, *who am I, and will I be enough now that my job as a full-time mother, my defining role, is ending?*

Various group members tried to reassure Anna that she would discover a new purpose for herself. They encouraged her to think about who she was before children and what activities had brought her joy back then. Some of the women reminded her that she was a wonderful mother and that she should be proud because she had raised wonderful children.

We did our best to lift her spirits and surround her in love.

And we all pledged to support and pray for her as she entered this new phase of life. But we didn't answer her question, *but who will I be?* And we didn't reassure her that she was enough.

I thought about Anna often over the next few days. I wondered what wisdom my grandmother would have had for her. I'm sure she would have made sure Anna knew she was loved by God and was surrounded by good friends. And she would have prayed for her daily.

The idea of *enough* also stayed with me. It floated through my mind as I wandered around the farm. It popped into my mind when I was drafting a will for a client. It especially rolled around when I wasn't expecting it. It was a quiet whisper that was never very far away. And it was a persistent whisper I knew I couldn't ignore.

At our next gathering, I sensed that another group member was facing a difficulty. When Sarah entered the room, I could tell she had been crying. Her eyes looked a bit red and puffy. The previous week, she had come to our meeting directly from work with her makeup still perfect. Today, she was wearing casual clothes, and she was not wearing any makeup. There was also a defeated air in the way she walked. There was something wrong, but she didn't say anything. When others shared prayer concerns, she remained quiet. And instead of engaging with the women who shared as she had done in the previous gathering, she stared at the floor. As soon as the meeting ended, I asked if I could show her something in the nearby kitchen. She agreed and followed me.

Once we were alone, I said, "I hope I'm not prying, but are you okay? You don't seem like yourself tonight."

She stared at me. It seemed she was weighing over whether she wanted to tell me what was happening. She stared at the floor and shifted her weight back and forth. Finally, she blurted out, "I lost my job yesterday. Downsized. Fired. Whatever you want to call it, I lost my job."

I felt the pain of her statement. "Oh, Sarah, I'm so sorry."

Tears filled her eyes and spilled down her cheeks. "I don't know what I'm going to do, Lydia. I poured myself into that company. I gave it my all. Plus, I have bills to pay. And then, all day I've been thinking," she said, pausing to wipe the tears from her face. "I keep thinking about Anna's question *but who will I be?* I don't know who I am without my career." She looked down at the floor again, but then she glanced up at me and asked, "Why wasn't I enough for them to keep me?"

I wanted to have words to help her feel better. I wanted to have a solution to her problem. I wanted to help, but I didn't know how. All I could do was be with her, praying that in some way, my presence helped her realize she wasn't alone. Her pain was so palpable that I fought to keep my own tears from falling. When her tears began to dry, I asked if I could offer a prayer for her. She nodded yes, and I prayed to the Lord for guidance and peace. I also thanked God for being with us even when we can't always sense His presence. After I finished, I said, "Sarah, I hope you know that none of us walk these journeys alone. I'm here anytime you need someone to talk to. I'm sorry I don't have answers, but I can listen."

"Thank you," she replied. "I think that's all anyone can do right now. At first, I didn't even want to come tonight, but for some reason I felt I had to. Sharing this burden with you makes it seem a bit easier. I think I just need to take things one day at a time. And knowing I have a caring friend helps. Thank you."

As I drove home, I thought about all the women I knew who had recently admitted that they didn't think they were enough. Their reasons for feeling that way varied, but the emotions were all the same. They believed their identities had been removed, and they all felt inadequate and unworthy. That something was missing for each of them. As I thought about it, I realized I had been in the same place not long ago. Then it occurred to me: perhaps I had not moved beyond that feeling either. *But who will I be?* Was that why I was struggling with my former business partner's news? Was it bothering me because I thought I wasn't enough or that I hadn't yet fully defined myself since stepping away from my career? Did this news trigger all those old feelings of being unworthy and unlovable?

All I had were questions. I would need time to think about all of this.

The discussions from our small group floated around in my brain for a couple of days. I eventually decided that journaling about the conversations with Anna, Sarah, Ellie, and Jordyn might help me sort through things, so I started by summarizing everything I could remember from each of those conversations. I then wrote about what I felt when I heard them express their deep feelings. Once I had written everything I could remember, I glanced at my work. This was emotional! I identified with each of these women in a different way.

Then something else occurred to me: I had been lost when I first returned home. And while it took time, prayer, hard emotional work, and the wisdom and guidance of various people in my life, I had finally realized the redemption of my past. This allowed me to step into a new future. I thought, after I had done all that work, I had arrived. I had a strong faith, and I knew God loved me. But now, looking over these notes, I recognized myself in each one of these women's stories, and I realized I had not arrived at all. I still felt lost or that something was missing in my life.

I didn't know what to think about this realization. When I sat down to pray, the thought that came to me was that I could not find answers on my own. I needed to tackle these topics with wisdom greater than my own, so I decided to call Gail. When she answered, I asked if she had time to discuss a deep subject.

"We could at least begin the conversation. If I need time to think about it, then we can find another time to continue," she suggested.

"That's fair," I said. "Lately, I've heard several women talk about how they feel inadequate. For various reasons, they don't think they are enough, and I don't know how to reassure them. I'm wondering if I'm struggling with knowing how to respond because I identify with their feelings of inadequacy."

"I think everyone struggles with this issue at least now and then."

"So, we have company."

"Yes. I know I've struggled at times, and I think most people do. As far as how to help them, I'll need to think about that," she told me.

"I understand. There's something else I want to talk about too. I thought I had faith figured out and that I was on the right path. Listening to these women, I'm beginning to doubt that. Maybe I don't have everything figured out."

"I'm sure you don't, Lydia. Our faith is a journey, not a destination. There will never be a time when you can truly say you have this figured out. You just won't. I believe we are meant to spend our entire lives learning about God and learning about ourselves. If we stop learning and growing, then we are stagnant, and that's not what God wants. There is no completion in our faith journey. There's only growth."

I wasn't sure how to respond. I'm the type of person who likes to master a subject. Conquer it. But I had the sudden realization that this would not be the case with faith.

"Gail, is it okay to doubt your faith?" I asked.

"I think it's perfectly normal to have doubts. And I will also add that doubts and questions are not sins. In fact, I think that God likes doubts and questions because they are simply an invitation to continue learning about Him and our faith."

"I guess the good news is that there isn't something wrong with me or my faith," I said.

"No, there isn't. You're normal. Are you still faithfully reading the Bible and praying?"

"Honestly? Not as often as I was."

"That's the first thing I would suggest. Get back to the basics. I remember you once told me how beneficial journaling was to you," she said.

"I just started doing that again," I told her.

"Good for you! Keep it up. Why don't we have dinner together soon and continue this conversation?"

"I would appreciate it. Thank you, my friend."

"Good night, Lydia. Fall asleep talking to God. That's the best advice I can give you this evening."

Falling asleep talking to God seemed like a wonderful suggestion. I went upstairs, climbed into my comfortable, antique canopy bed, and did just that. I fell asleep talking to God.

Chapter 12

THE NEXT MORNING, I woke up well rested, but with questions still on my mind. I thought about my conversation with Gail. I liked what she'd said about our doubts and questions being invitations to learn and grow. I decided to put that idea into action and spent time reading and praying. I quickly realized that this would be a wonderful way to begin each morning. The peace I felt while praying was very comforting. After eating breakfast, I began my workday.

Ellie called while I was responding to a few emails. It had been a few days since we had talked, so I was pleased to catch up with her. She filled me in on her new job, and then she told me the purpose of her call.

"Lydia, I've made my decision. I want to file for divorce," she said.

"I'm sure it was a difficult decision for you," I replied.

"It's a decision that has been in the making for years. I didn't have the courage before. I was always worried about Jordyn and money. Since Jordyn is older now, I think she can process it. In fact, she asked me the other night what I was waiting for. She said she never remembered her dad treating me with respect, and that reinforced the idea that this marriage was not a positive example for her. I know now that I can provide for us, so it seems the time is right. What I need is a lawyer, and I want you to represent me."

"Ellie, I'm honored you thought of me, but I've not handled many divorce cases. And to be honest, the few cases that I've worked on didn't involve minor children or one of the parties being a business owner. Your case will be more complicated than what I've done before."

"Everybody knows what a great job you did in the water case. You stood up to those lawyers when the city wanted to drill a well out here that would have dried up our individual wells. You did your research, and you stood up to them. Sam says he was amazed watching you. He said you were fierce and didn't back down. You stood up to them and took care of all of us. That's what I need now—someone who will stand up and fight for me."

I felt my eyes get misty. The water case had been a tough battle, but for me personally, it went beyond being a battle over water rights. It was instrumental in helping me discover God's purpose for my life. After winning the case, I realized that my purpose was to bring comfort to people, specifically to my community of neighbors and friends by helping them when they needed legal advice. Wasn't that what Ellie was asking me to do—to bring her comfort during what would be a very difficult time for her and her daughter? I took a deep breath and lifted a quick prayer asking God for guidance. This time, God's answer was swift and clear. *Yes.*

"Ellie, I will do my very best for you," I said.

"Oh, Lydia, you are truly an answer to my prayers. Thank you!"

"I'm going to be honest. Since I've never worked on a case like this, your divorce may not be a quick process for you."

"I understand. I'm not in a rush. It just feels good to have made the decision and to have taken the first step."

My research on Ellie's case began with calling a few attorneys I knew who practiced family law. I was glad I had stayed in at least casual contact with them. I asked them questions concerning any potential issues we would face pertaining to Clark's family-owned business and about any other topics they thought might arise. One attorney I called was Kate, a law school classmate. After we briefly caught up on our careers since we finished law school, I shared the purpose of my call. I told her about Ellie's case and why I needed some guidance on how to proceed. She gave me some helpful advice, and then she said, "I feel that there might be more to this case than what you have shared."

"You're correct," I told her. "It's a sad situation. I'm afraid this woman has also been verbally and emotionally abused. When she first shared her story with me, I did some research on domestic violence. It was eye opening and very upsetting."

"I can hear the genuine care in your voice for this woman. Have you ever considered volunteering with a domestic violence shelter or with an organization that works with rape survivors? I ask because survivors benefit when they have an ally to support them through the process of a court case, which can be a lonely venture for a woman who has already faced betrayal and trauma."

"No, I hadn't thought of doing that, but it does sound like something I would be interested in and passionate about. I will investigate that. Thank you for the suggestion and thank you for sharing your time and knowledge with me."

"You're welcome. It was good to hear from you. Be sure to let me know if you decide to volunteer."

I spent most of the week working on Ellie's case, and I realized my energy was drained. I needed a distraction. I needed to clear my mind before I burned out, so I decided to call Gail to see if she would like to go shopping with me. We agreed to meet on Saturday.

We spent the drive to the mall catching up. She filled me in on what she was currently teaching and a little about some of her students. The conversation was light and exactly what I needed after all my research and difficult conversations with Ellie. It was stressful to witness the end of a marriage even though I knew Ellie was making the correct decision for Jordyn and herself.

When we arrived at my favorite clothing store, Gail asked what I was looking for.

"Since I've made my health a priority by eating better and walking, I've noticed some of my clothes are too big," I explained.

"Making your health a priority is always a good decision," Gail said. "And it's a great idea to have some new clothes that fit properly."

"I must confess that although I know I've lost a little weight, I don't see it. I just know that some of my clothes are baggier than they used to be, so I thought I should find something now while I have time to look."

"Good idea. And since the styles are always changing, you never know when you'll find something you like."

Gail convinced me to try on a few dresses even though I didn't think they would be flattering on me. The first dress I came out of the dressing room wearing was one that was quite formfitting.

It was knee-length and sapphire blue. The cut of the dress was wider at the shoulders and was cinched tight at the waistline with decorative beading on the left side. The cut of the dress naturally accentuated my bust.

Since puberty, I had received comments from boys about my bust. Even before I had been sexually assaulted, their comments made me uncomfortable, but after the rape, I perceived these comments as another violation. Their remarks seemed to be yet another example that I was only a body that someone could abuse. I was sure they wouldn't have said those things if they'd seen me as a person instead.

Because of my past experiences, I usually wore only loose-fitting clothing. Besides, I had always been slightly heavier than my peers, and I didn't think I looked as good as they did in tighter-fitting clothing. I knew this dress wasn't tight, but it was more formfitting than I was typically drawn to. And if I was being honest with myself, after I was raped, I didn't want to wear any clothes that accentuated my body. I had wanted to hide. I took a deep breath and braced myself as I stepped out of the dressing room.

"Oh, Lydia, you look amazing! That dress is perfect for you. The color and the fit are perfect. You truly look stunning!" Gail exclaimed.

"What?" I asked, surprised at her reaction.

"You can't look at yourself in the mirror and tell me that you don't think that dress looks good on you."

I glanced down at the dress for a minute and then looked up at Gail. "I don't see myself as the woman you're seeing."

Gail's eyes grew wide, and she raised her eyebrows at me.

And then she said, "If you don't buy that dress, I'm going to buy it for you."

"If you're sure it looks okay, I guess I will."

We finished our shopping and then left the mall. Once we were back in the car and driving home, Gail turned to me and said, "Okay, we need to talk. I didn't say anything in the store because I knew this needed to be a private conversation, but . . . were you serious that you didn't think you looked wonderful in the dress?"

"I was serious," I told her.

"Lydia, that's an old recording playing in your head. Of course, a person is beautiful regardless of their size, but I know how hard you've been working at improving your health. It's okay to acknowledge that. And it's okay to purchase an outfit that fits nicely and complements the effort you have put into yourself."

I was glad Gail was driving because I could feel a lump forming in my throat, and I felt my heart begin to race. Body image was a difficult topic for me. It was another painful subject from my past that I had tried to block instead of facing. I could see Gail glancing over at me out of the corner of my eye, so I decided to tell her what I was feeling.

"I've never felt comfortable in my own skin. I was never thin like other girls, and so I was often taunted by my peers. I also entered puberty earlier than anyone else my age, which just increased the upsetting comments and cruel jokes. So, at the point in life when we are often the most self-conscious, I began to hate the way I looked. To make matters worse, I was also the girl who didn't know anything about fashion or makeup or hair styles. And shopping to find clothes that fit properly and meet my grandmother's standards was a battle and not something

I enjoyed. I suppose I still view myself as the girl who doesn't measure up regarding my appearance."

Gail sighed. "My friend, I'm so sorry you faced that type of shaming. Though you can't go back and change what happened, you can work on replacing those old thoughts that try to tell you that you're not beautifully made. Because you are! God made you to be extraordinary, and I think you are stepping into that word in other areas. Your self-image just needs to catch up."

I nodded in agreement. "I just reread one of Grandmother's lessons, and part of what she wrote said that we cannot fully accept God's healing if we continue to listen to the old recordings from our past. She ended by saying it was time for me to listen to new ones that tell me God loves me."

Gail smiled. "Your grandmother is still sharing her wisdom with you even after being gone for over a year. I'm not surprised. I love her wisdom."

"There's something else too," I said.

"What's that?"

"After I was raped, I didn't want to wear any clothes that showed off my figure. I felt that showing my figure would be an invitation to more unwanted advances."

Gail took one hand off the steering wheel and squeezed my hand. "I'm so sorry for your pain. I hope you know that your rape wasn't your fault. It had nothing to do with what clothing you were wearing. Rape is about power. Not clothes."

I nodded. I understood what she was saying, but a voice deep inside me asked, *but do you believe it wasn't your fault?*

She continued. "If there's any chance that you think it was your fault at all, that's another old recording that needs to be replaced." She glanced over at me to see if I was hearing her words.

I sighed as I thought about how difficult it was to replace those old "tapes" in my head. There was an abundance of them, and most played only a negative message.

"I have no idea how to replace these old recordings with new ones," I admitted.

"Sure you do," Gail said, "but it will take time and effort, as do all worthwhile things."

I sighed again and looked out the window. Time and effort.

Gail's words stayed with me for the rest of the day. God had made me to be extraordinary, and I was stepping into that word in some areas of my life. I now wondered about what areas she thought I was doing that. Perhaps she was thinking about my continued growth in my faith, or maybe she meant my efforts to help Ellie. It occurred to me that I should just ask her instead of wondering what she meant.

I did, however, understand her comment that my self-image needed to catch up to my new life and honor the idea that God had made each of us to be extraordinary. I had always battled with self-image, and I had never looked like the women that the media portrayed as being ideal. The shame and pain from my trauma that had been my companions for most of my life also contributed to my low self-esteem. Yes, I had heard what Gail said about changing the recordings I listened to. But even though *she* felt confident that I knew how to change them, I still was not sure how.

Chapter 13

THE DAY AFTER THE SHOPPING TRIP had been busy, so I hadn't had time to think about how to change my negative thoughts. I returned to thinking about this topic as I drank my morning coffee on Monday. Aunt Lu watched me with a furrowed brow. She didn't say anything, but she kept her eye on me as she was working. I could tell she was concerned that I seemed lost in my coffee cup. Eventually, she asked if I would go to Mrs. Dalton's farm and buy some fresh eggs. She was in the middle of baking and couldn't leave to get them. One of the blessings I had rediscovered since moving back to the farm was the delight of fresh eggs. My friends who had never tasted the difference between a fresh egg and one that sat in a store for a long time had no idea what they were missing.

Mrs. Dalton was one of my grandmother's dear friends, and I always loved going to visit her. As I drove to her farm, I remembered my visit with her not long after Grandmother had died. I had not yet made my decision to relocate here. When I'd told Mrs. Dalton that I didn't want to leave, she'd said the reason I felt drawn to stay was because I had the farm in my blood. I wasn't sure that was true at the time, but I had grown very fond of the peace and tranquility here. I cringed when I remembered my comment to Mrs. Dalton about how I was surprised she was still milking her own cows when she was in her late eighties. She'd informed me that she wasn't dead yet. Chuckling to myself, I vowed not to say anything disrespectful on this visit regardless of what farm chores I found her doing.

I saw her come around the house on her riding lawn mower as I pulled into the driveway. I decided then and there that I wanted to be like Mrs. Dalton when I "grew up." She was simply amazing.

She pulled up alongside my car and shut off the mower. "Did you come to get eggs for your aunt?" she asked when I rolled down my window.

"Yes, I did, Mrs. Dalton."

"Well, let's go inside and get them, but first, I need some coffee and a cinnamon roll. I pulled the rolls out of the oven right before I started to mow. I'm guessing they are still warm." Then she squinted and took a long look at me. "By the looks of you, you need one too. Isn't your aunt feeding you?"

"Yes, ma'am, she is, but I've been trying to eat healthy and maybe lose a little weight. She was feeding me too well."

"Hmm. Seems to me you might be overdoing that."

"Overdoing what?"

"Weight loss. Just think about this. Eating healthy doesn't always result in weight loss, and weight loss isn't always healthy."

I smiled at her. "Yes, ma'am." Then I rolled up the window and got out of the car.

In the kitchen, Mrs. Dalton started the coffee maker and brought out two plates for the cinnamon rolls. It looked like I was going to enjoy one regardless of whether it was healthy or not.

When we sat down at the table, Mrs. Dalton looked right at me. "Well, how do you like being back on the farm?"

"I'm very happy. I enjoy the quiet and the less frantic pace."

"Seems like you're holding something back," she said, squinting at me again.

I couldn't believe how intuitive she was. I took a sip of coffee, debating about what to share. I decided I could use another opinion on what had been bothering me, so I told her about the phone call from my former partner and about how I couldn't let it go. I explained that there was something about his decision that upset me, but I couldn't accurately define it. I told her that he would be earning a high salary, and I was working hard for myself, but I was barely making any money at all.

Mrs. Dalton was silent as I shared, and she watched me intently. It occurred to me that she was not simply listening to be polite but truly listening to me, and I remembered something my grandmother always said. God gave us two ears and only one mouth, so we should do twice as much listening as we do talking. Even with that wisdom, I knew I often only listened with one ear most of the time. Mrs. Dalton was honoring me with the gift of her full attention.

When I finished my story, she held her cup in her hands but didn't drink. She looked out the window for a minute, and then she turned to look at me. I felt like she was trying to peer into my soul.

"Honey, it sounds like you are doubting your decision," she said.

"Perhaps."

"What makes you doubt it? When you made the decision to stay, it seemed you were sure about it. Why doubt now?"

"I just can't let that conversation go. I keep remembering it."

"Are you a little jealous? Sounds like that man is making an awful lot of money, and you said you're struggling."

"I thought about that. I know that might be part of it, but I don't think that's the whole problem. It just seems like it's something deeper."

"Do you need a new challenge? Maybe what he has planned seems exciting, and you're in need of a new adventure."

"Oh, I seem to have found plenty of adventure lately."

"Ah, I see. So, you can't figure it out, but you just can't let that phone call go," she said in a matter-of-fact tone. The way she said that seemed like she had a suspicion of what was going on in my head, but she didn't want to say it aloud.

Finally, I asked her, "Do you think I made a mistake?"

"Does it matter what anyone thinks but you?" she asked.

"No, I suppose not."

She gave me a knowing nod. "But I will say it seems like you're searching for something."

I took another sip of my coffee. What could I be searching for? I replayed the phone conversation and this conversation with Mrs. Dalton again in my head. I thought about the women in my group at church—about Anna's questions and Sarah's concerns. Time seemed to stop as I sat there, remembering and thinking. Then I blurted out, "Mrs. Dalton, do you think I'm enough?"

She set her cup down and said, "Well, now we're getting somewhere. Is that what this is about? It's not doubts about your decision to relocate. It's doubts about yourself. I know I'm not your grandmother, but she was my very dear friend for more years than you've been alive. I feel confident that I know what she would say to you, so I'm going to say it.

"Now, listen well—you are enough. You are a child of God, and that means you are enough. You don't have to prove anything. God made you. Case closed. It doesn't matter what I think or what anyone else thinks. God knows you are enough. And now, you need to believe it too. Did you hear me?"

Tears welled in my eyes. Listening to Mrs. Dalton was just like listening to my grandmother. I missed her deeply, but I was so thankful that Grandmother's friend knew what I needed to hear. I wiped away my tears and eventually spoke again.

"Thank you for sharing your wisdom with me."

She patted my arm. "Honey, we are all in this life together. We must share our love and our wisdom with one other."

I smiled. A compatible silence fell between us until I glanced at the kitchen clock and realized how long we'd been sitting. I swallowed the last sip of my coffee and then said, "I better get those eggs and get back before Aunt Lu needs them."

Mrs. Dalton set her mug on the table and moved to rise from her chair. "I don't want to hold her up, so I suppose you better get moving."

As I climbed into my car with the egg cartons in my hand, Mrs. Dalton called out to me from her porch. "Don't be a stranger, honey. I want to hear all about you realizing that you're enough."

"Yes, ma'am," I said, giving her a wave. "I will come again."

Our conversation played on repeat in my mind as I went about my day. It was exactly what I'd needed to hear. I thanked God not just for my grandmother but also for Mrs. Dalton and for all the other wise people in my life.

One of the concepts that filled my mind was that of doubt. I thought about Gail's viewpoint that God likes doubts and questions. She had also said that faith is a journey and not a destination, and that is why doubts and questions lead us to learning and growing. I smiled as I thought about these ideas. As a lifelong learner, I was pleased that these were other concepts I could explore.

And then my thoughts turned to the concept of being enough. This had multiple facets, ranging from *having* enough to *being* enough. Some people based their feelings of being enough on their earthly possessions, whereas others focused on their physical appearances. Though I had struggled with body image, I knew I viewed my career as the primary basis of my self-worth. I realized that I had based my worth more on the prestige and power of my career and less on my salary. Lately, it seemed that I had fallen back into old habits with that thinking. When I decided to move back home, this decision had been based on a purpose of bringing comfort to others through my career as a lawyer. But hearing from my partner had, in part, triggered those old habits. It reminded me of the prestige and power I had left behind. And I started refocusing on those values instead of on why I had left it all behind in the first place.

My recent conversations with all the people who had voiced concerns about their own worth reinforced those same feelings in myself. These thoughts had haunted me, and asking Mrs. Dalton about them was the first time I had voiced this aloud.

She was correct when she said I wasn't simply doubting my decisions; I was doubting myself and my worth. I knew she was also correct that God's love and acceptance was a much better way to define my self-worth. This concept would require time to process both because it was complex and because there were numerous lies tied to it. Working to untangle all my thoughts and beliefs around this idea was yet another part of my life's journey.

Because Sam and I had both been busy, there had not been much time to catch up about how the planting season was progressing. We had played phone tag for several days until I finally decided to take a drive to see if I could find him. The fields I owned were spread over several miles, so it took time, but I eventually found him planting. He was in the middle of one of the fields and was far enough away that I couldn't see his face, but I knew when he saw my car because he stopped the tractor in the middle of the row, jumped down, and headed over to where I waited.

It was unusual for me to show up unannounced, so naturally, he was concerned something was wrong. Worry covered his face as he walked up to me, but I gave him a reassuring smile and held up a thermos in one hand and a foil-wrapped plate in another.

"We've both been so busy, we haven't had much time to talk lately. I just wanted to catch up and get an update on how things are going," I told him.

He immediately looked relieved. "I'm sorry, Lydia," he said. "I haven't done a good job of keeping up with you."

"No worries. I know you've been busy. That's why I decided to come to you. I brought some coffee and some of Aunt Lu's cookies if you'd like to take a break and chat."

"That sounds good. I could sure use some cookies."

We sat on the hood of my car, and Sam caught me up on the status of each field and what still needed to be completed. It felt good to know that everything was on schedule. I'd been a little concerned that he might be behind because of the extra responsibilities and stress that Ellie's situation was creating for him, but that was not the case. He was on top of everything.

After we had finished discussing business, I decided to change the subject. "How is Ellie doing?"

"She seems good most of the time, but every now and then, I can hear her crying. I know this isn't how she thought her life would go. We were raised to think marriage is forever, so this is hard on her."

I nodded. "And how is Jordyn?"

He shrugged. "She doesn't say much. I think she's even quieter than I am. Who knows what's going through that girl's head? I can't imagine being her age and going through this. But I will say—she notices everything. Ellie tries to hide problems from her, but I think Jordyn knows exactly what's going on. There's no doubt she knew how her mom was being treated."

"Maybe I should think of something Jordyn and I can do together. She opened up to me a little one of the times we were together. I'm not sure what we'll do, but I'll plan to spend some time with her again."

"That would be great, Lydia. Thanks." He grinned. "Now, can I change the subject?"

"Of course."

"When are you going to sing at church again?"

I laughed. "What? Wow, that certainly is changing the subject! Why would you want to hear me sing anyway?"

"Hey, don't put yourself down. You have a nice voice. And you always seem to find songs that speaks to what we need to hear."

I'm sure I blushed every shade of red. I didn't think I had a good singing voice, and given my feelings about Sam, the compliment hit me harder than I would have expected. I hoped he hadn't noticed how uncomfortable I was. All I could say was, "Thank you. You are kind to say that. I don't have a song in mind that I could share, but I'll think about it."

"I hope you do. Now, boss lady, I need to get back to work."

I chuckled and added, "Yes, you do."

He thanked me for the coffee and cookies and walked back to the tractor. I got in my car and watched Sam climb back into the tractor before waving goodbye. As I drove home, I realized I truly enjoyed visiting with Sam. He was a gentle soul who had a way of putting people at ease—except when he paid compliments that made me blush.

Chapter 14

THE GARDEN HAD BEEN NEGLECTED. I had been so busy with other things that I was behind on planting the huge garden that Aunt Lu and I enjoyed. She could no longer handle the stooping and kneeling involved in planting, weeding, and harvesting, so it was up to me to do it. She took the lead, however, when it came to canning and freezing our bounty. I lacked the skills needed for canning, because it made me nervous. I always envisioned the pressure cooker exploding and sending the contents flying off into the air and was grateful for Aunt Lu's talents in this regard. When I got back to the farmhouse after visiting Sam, I headed out to the garden to give it the TLC it needed.

It felt like I had been working in the garden for an eternity by the time that Aunt Lu came to my rescue to tell me that Reverend Peters was on the phone. On our way back to the house, I asked her how long I had been working. She told me that it had been only about an hour, but I was sure it had been considerably longer. Maybe gardening was like working in dog years: if one "dog year" was equal to seven human years, then perhaps one minute of garden work was really like an hour. At least, my tired body felt that way.

"Hello, Reverend Peters. I'm sorry it took me so long to come to the phone," I said. Grinning, I added, "Aunt Lu had to drag me away from the garden."

I could hear the smile in his voice as he replied. "Lu warned me it would take a minute. I do apologize for interrupting your work."

I laughed. "Trust me, Reverend Peters, I was ready to stop."

He chuckled too and said, "I'm glad I could give you an excuse for a break. I wanted to touch base about your small group. We always need ways to connect with each other, and I'm so glad you and Gail started this."

"We're glad to do it. We seem to have developed a good rapport with the other members. Personally, I look forward to our gatherings."

"I'm glad to hear it. Is there anything I can help with?" he asked.

"I don't think so, but I may take you up on that at some point."

"I'm happy to help at any time. Oh, and while I've got you on the phone, I also wanted to ask when you would be willing to share some special music again. I know everyone enjoys it when you sing."

I laughed again. "Did Sam put you up to asking this?"

"No," he said. I could tell by the way he answered that he had no idea what I was talking about. "Why do you ask?"

"Oh, it's just funny timing. Sam just asked me when I was going to sing again at church. Do you have a song suggestion, if I were to agree?"

"No. Whatever you would like is fine. What Sunday may I put you down for?"

I silently sighed. Oh, why not? "Might as well make it this Sunday."

"Perfect. Thank you, Lydia."

After I hung up the phone, I wondered why I hadn't given myself a little more time to think of something to share.

Sunday seemed to arrive quickly. Sam's comment that my song choice always said what people needed to hear added extra stress for me. What message did people need to hear? Instead of worrying about that, I finally decided to focus on what message I needed to hear. With all the turmoil and challenging topics that had been floating around me, I longed for stillness in my soul. So, I decided to sing "Be Still, My Soul." I found the melody haunting, and the lyrics seemed appropriate. After the sermon, I stood up to sing the special music for the day.

Be still, my soul; the Lord is on your side;
Bear patiently the cross of grief or pain;
Leave to your God to order and provide;
In ev'ry change he faithful will remain.
Be still, my soul; your best, your heav'nly friend
Through thorny ways leads to a joyful end.

Be still, my soul; your God will undertake
To guide the future as he has the past;
Your hope, your confidence, let nothing shake;
All now mysterious shall be bright at last.
Be still, my soul; the waves and winds still know
His voice who ruled them while he lived below

> *Be still, my soul; the hour is hastning on*
> *When we shall be forever with the Lord*
> *When disappointment, grief, and fear are gone,*
> *Sorrow forgot, love's purest joys restored.*
> *Be still my soul; when change and tears are past,*
> *All safe and blessed we shall meet at last.*

After the service, Sam came up to me with a grin on his face. "Did you already have that planned when I asked you about singing?"

"No, I didn't, but the same day you asked, Reverend Peters called and also asked me to sing. His timing surprised me, and I agreed before I knew what I was saying."

"I enjoyed it, and I wanted you to know. That's what I was saying to you. Somehow, you always have the right message. I needed to hear 'Be Still, My Soul,' and I know others did too. I think Ellie especially needed it. She started crying and left during the final hymn. She still has problems to work through."

"Yes, she does."

"Well, I need to go and see if Ellie is okay. Thanks again, Lydia," he said, nodding to me as he walked away.

"You're welcome. And if Ellie needs something, let me know."

Sam waved an acknowledgment and left the building. I gathered my things and went to find Aunt Lu.

Aunt Lu and I stuffed ourselves with a fabulous Sunday meal of roasted chicken and sweet potato casserole. After we finished washing and putting away the dishes, I excused myself to my room. I had wanted to journal since my conversation with Mrs. Dalton, but I had not made the time to do that.

Journaling my thoughts and feelings was often hard work. It was challenging to face my emotions and try to find the words to describe what I was feeling. But the idea of being enough was so important that I knew I needed to put the work in.

I have been in a funk since my former business partner called to tell me he's closing the business and taking a different job. I've been experiencing a variety of emotions, and they are all negative. Anger. Perhaps jealousy. Doubt. Actually, a long list of doubts. I've also felt a sense of being lost or searching for something. Recently, I've even wondered if I'm enough. Is feeling inadequate at the root of everything else? When Mrs. Dalton and I talked about this, she said I'm enough because I'm a child of God. I don't have to prove anything to God because He made me and loves me. Then she said that God knows I'm enough and that now I need to know it and believe it too. It's easy to write those words, but it's not as easy to sincerely believe it.

I've known people who base their self-worth on the possessions they own or want to own. They think they will be happy or perhaps accepted if they drive a certain vehicle or buy a bigger house. Then there are people who base their self-worth on their appearances, and they spend a great deal of money trying to meet society's definition of beauty. I have certainly battled a negative self-image, and I know I still have work to do to face those issues. But I also wonder about self-worth beyond possessions and appearance. What about wondering if I'm enough in my career? Am I fully utilizing my God-given talents? Am I fulfilling my God-given purpose? Can I ever fully live the life God designed for me? How can I ever be enough at that?

I stopped writing and held my pen just above the paper. There was another question that needed to be addressed. I began to write again.

Can I be enough considering my past traumas? This question is difficult to face. I have based a significant part of my self-worth on what happened in my past. Not only being raped but also the multitude of poor choices I made afterward. I lived in darkness for years because of those events and decisions. Intellectually, I know the violent actions of others should not play a role in my concept of being enough, and yet it has. How do I move past these traumas informing my self-worth? Where do I even begin?

I reread what I had written. *Am I enough?* I knew my answer should be based on how God would answer that question. I knew that, but I also knew it would take time for me to believe it and live it.

Chapter 15

TIME WAS FLYING BY. Once again, it was time for our women's small group to meet. I continued to be surprised by the joy and comfort I received from this group. I had never realized how deeply I needed a community of other women to share and learn with. They had become like family to me, even in the short time we'd been meeting together. I wondered how Anna and Sarah were doing, so I decided to speak to each of them privately after our session. I was confident that Sarah had shared her job loss only with me, and I didn't want to say anything about it in front of the group.

As the other women arrived and we began our meeting, I realized I was not the only person who had been thinking about Anna. A woman named Margaret also mentioned that she'd been thinking of her.

"You've continued to be on my mind," Margaret said. "When you asked, 'But who will I be?' I completely resonated with that. I thought the same thing when I retired from teaching. Who would I be without my teaching career? And sending your baby off to college"—she took a deep breath—"that is so hard. I think people, and women specifically, need to talk more about this. You aren't alone in wondering about how to define yourself in the future or wondering if you are still enough without the role that defined you."

Tears welled in Anna eyes. "Thank you for saying that. You've all been so kind and supportive. I felt so foolish after I blurted that out. I thought I was being insecure and ridiculous."

We all reassured Anna that she was not insecure, and she wasn't ridiculous, either. What she was feeling was legitimate.

Gail added, "The fact that we don't talk about these things makes us believe we are alone in feeling this way and that something must be wrong with us, but nothing could be further from the truth. These transitions are challenging, and we need to work through them. Over time, you'll find a new way to define yourself because you have an abundance of gifts that can be used in a variety of ways. But while you explore this new definition, keep reminding yourself there is nothing wrong with you. You are on life's journey."

Anna nodded. "Thanks again, everyone. I appreciate it. I told my husband about what I'd shared. You won't believe what he quoted to me. He said, 'Anna, did you ever see the movie *Cool Runnings* about the Jamaican bobsled team?' I told him I've never even heard of it. Anyway, he went on to tell me one of the lines in the movie. 'A gold medal is a wonderful thing. But if you're not enough without one, you'll never be enough with one.' At first, I didn't quite understand what he was trying to say. But then he told me, 'Honey, you're enough whether you've got babies at home or they are all grown up. Being enough is about who you *are* not what you *do*.'" She smiled at the memory.

Gail grinned too and said, "That's an amazing line. I might have to go watch that movie now. And it sounds to me like you have an incredibly wise husband. He's given me something to think about. I also think we often place our self-worth on doing and achieving things, but I don't think that serves us well. There will always be the next thing to acquire or the next goal to accomplish."

The others nodded. A few even added some verbal *amens*. We then turned to the book we were reading and had a great discussion. When the meeting was over, I realized Sarah had slipped out before I could talk to her.

Driving home, I reflected on the quote Anna had mentioned from *Cool Runnings*. If you're not enough without a gold medal, then you won't be enough with one. If you're an Olympic athlete and a gold medal doesn't make you realize that you're enough, then what in the world could make you enough? Ah. Maybe there was something in that phrase, *what in the world*. It's not something from this world that would make you enough or complete. I knew Mrs. Dalton had a big piece of the puzzle figured out.

As children of God, we are enough. I remembered Gail's statement from our group session, saying that we often place our self-worth on doing and achieving things, and it doesn't serve us well. I had proof of that in my own life. I had been quite successful in my past career, and I'd worked with some powerful people, and yet, I knew something was missing. If I wasn't enough with everything I had achieved in that career, then I don't think I could ever be enough in any career. Then I remembered what else Anna's husband said—that being enough is about who you are, not what you do.

The conversation tonight had given me a great deal to think about concerning my own life. It's amazing that someone who shared something so personal caused us all to stop and realize that her concerns were also our own concerns. I wasn't alone in wondering if I was enough. And the idea of basing my self-worth on who I am as a child of God instead of on my career or what role I hold was a paradigm shift for me that would take time to process.

Chapter 16

EVEN THOUGH MY SCHEDULE was busy with growing my own law practice and volunteering with the small group at church, I felt the nudge to support hurting women in our community. I continued to reflect on the phone call I'd had about this with my law school colleague, when she had suggested volunteering with a group that supports domestic violence or sexual assault survivors, and I could not let that idea go. I made some phone calls to learn about different organizations, and I didn't have to look far to find a local office. These crimes were not limited to large cities. Unfortunately, they occur everywhere.

The organization I decided to volunteer with supported both domestic violence survivors and victims of sexual assault. When I arrived for my first training session, I met the local director who led the introductory session. She shared numerous statistics about domestic violence and sexual assault, and she also shared what role we would have as volunteers. She told us we would be responsible for sharing the details of the court system, including the steps of the trial, what to expect at each step, and the dates when the client would need to be in attendance. Our primary responsibility, though, was to be an ally before, during, and after the court proceedings. It was made clear that we were not therapists, but we were an ally. We were also responsible for connecting our clients with the variety of other resources the organization offered. The next speaker discussed trauma in general and then went into specifics regarding domestic violence and sexual assault.

Intellectually, I knew the training would trigger memories of my rape and how I had responded to it over the years. I was surprised at how intensely I felt the emotional pain, and how I physically felt the pain even now. I took deep, slow breaths to control my breathing and my racing heart, and I constantly reminded myself that I was not in danger. I was remembering what had happened in the past, and those memories didn't understand that I was not in danger now. There were a few times throughout the session when I thought about leaving, and I was proud of myself for staying. But when I reached my car at the end of the day, I felt exhausted.

I kept thinking of Jordyn and Ellie and about everything they had been going through. Even though I was tired, I decided to drop by Sam's house to see if Jordyn was home. I was thrilled when she opened the front door.

"Hi, Jordyn. I'm in the mood to take a long hike and would love some company. Would you be interested in going with me? Maybe we can even end up at my house and see what cookies we can find."

"Sure, why not?" she replied, stepping outside and closing the door behind her. "It's not like there's anything else to do around here."

"Yeah. I remember thinking this was the most boring place on earth when I was your age," I said.

"You escaped from this place! Why did you come back?" she asked.

"It's a very long story. I'm afraid it would bore you even more than you are now. Someday, though, if you want to hear about it, I'll tell you all the details. In a nutshell, my priorities changed, and it turns out that this boring, quiet community fit those new priorities perfectly."

Jordyn looked at me with disbelief, her eyes wide. I'm sure she thought I was another crazy adult that she didn't want to end up being like. We walked for at least a mile without saying anything else, and I finally realized I was going to have to be the one to get this conversation moving.

"So, how are you really doing? Are you adjusting to living at Sam's and having your mom working?"

She shrugged. "I guess."

My experience with teenagers exclusively consisted of helping in Gail's classroom a few times. Getting Jordyn to share her thoughts and feelings with me continued to be challenging. And I was expecting tough!

"Jordyn, I hope you know I am a safe adult for you. That means you can share things with me, and they'll stay between just us. In my own life, I've often found it's nice to bounce ideas off other people. Get their thoughts. See if what they have to say helps me at all."

Silence.

Changing tactics, I decided to broach a subject that might have helped me when I was her age.

"So, I know we talked about emotions one time, but I was remembering that not so long ago, I thought it was wrong or bad to have big emotions. I used to be so angry I thought I would explode. For some reason, I thought that meant there was something wrong with me. It was like a river flowed through me, just under the surface. Or maybe it was more like a river of lava, and I thought it might erupt at any moment."

Jordyn stopped walking. She didn't say anything, but she stopped and looked at me.

"Do you ever feel like that?" I prompted.

"Yeah. And if I do anything that shows a little anger, I'm always being told to calm down," she said.

"How do you feel when someone says to calm down?"

"It makes me even angrier."

"Me too, Jordyn. Me too. We're entitled to our emotions. We do, however, need to learn how to think about, process, and release those emotions and energy in a positive way." I paused for a moment as I gathered my thoughts. "You know, Jesus had big emotions too. There are scriptures that tell us he cried. And do you know the story about when he overturned the tables in the temple? He was so angry that people were taking advantage of others that he overturned their tables. I'm not sure I would recommend doing that as a strategy now, but it does show us that Jesus also had big feelings."

She started walking again. "I hadn't thought of that, but I do remember the story."

"So, if it's okay for Jesus to have emotions and show them, don't you think it's okay for us too?" I asked.

"I guess so, but you said we need to release the energy in a positive way. How do you do that?"

"You need to experiment to see what will work for you. What works for me might not work for you, but here are some ideas. What we're doing right now is one of the best strategies for me, exercising. Remember how I also said that you need to process your emotions? When I'm walking, I think about what I'm feeling.

Frequently, what I think I'm feeling at first ends up not being it at all. Sometimes I think I feel angry, but when I start digging into it, I discover that I'm actually feeling sad or afraid instead. So I ask myself questions to learn more about what I'm feeling. Walking helps me think, and it also gets some of the physical energy of big emotions out too. Plus, all this beautiful nature is good for whatever is ailing me."

"What if you can't go for a walk?" she asked.

"It's always good to have multiple strategies that work for you. For example, I also like to write. I have a journal where I write about what I'm feeling. Things I'm sad or mad or scared about. Anything. Sometimes when I'm writing, I find I can't stop because ideas keep flowing out. I always feel better after I write. Some other ideas might be taking a bath or even punching a pillow. Be careful with that one, though. You don't want to break something or yourself!"

Finally, a smile from a teenager.

"I know I mentioned several things to think about, but I hope some of it helps," I told her.

She was quiet for a moment but then asked, "Do you still get angry?"

"Yes, I do. I think everyone feels anger, at least occasionally. It's how we process it or handle it that's different. Some people hide it deep down inside. Other people just explode with it. I don't think either of those is good. You need to discover a better approach for yourself."

"What makes you angry?"

"Oh, different things. Like when I see someone taking advantage of or harming another person or any of God's creations. And sometimes issues I've dealt with in my past pop up in a memory, and I need to work through things again." I paused, realizing how long I'd been talking. Then I said, "Listen to me just going on and on. What I want you to hear is that having emotions is normal."

"I understand," she said. "I'm glad to know I'm normal."

"You're absolutely perfect, Jordyn."

She smiled and looked at the ground. "Hey, Lydia? Do you think we could go see if your aunt baked cookies again?"

I laughed. "We sure can! All this walking has made me hungry."

We drove to my house and found Aunt Lu cleaning up the kitchen after making her famous sugar cookies. She was thrilled to spoil Jordyn with some cookies. Jordyn raved about how wonderful they were, and Aunt Lu asked if she would like to learn how to bake. I was surprised when Jordyn practically screamed yes in reply. It was exciting to see her so excited about something. Plus, it meant I would be able to spend more time with her. On the way back to Sam's house, Jordyn thanked me for coming over.

"You're welcome, Jordyn. I enjoy spending time with you. And Aunt Lu will be so thrilled to share all her baking secrets with you."

"I think it will be fun. Plus, I'm bored just watching TV."

"And we get to eat cookies when we're done!" I added.

Jordyn laughed. "I was thinking that too."

I wondered if I'd said too much to Jordyn on our walk, but then I also thought of other things I could have added to the conversation. Maybe someday I should tell her that anger can fill our hearts so full, it's a challenge to give and receive love. It's not that anger is bad, but it can become a problem if it's ignored. I also reflected on how anger and other big emotions still sneak in and haunt me at times. Judgment of myself and perceived judgment from society always seemed to be lurking under the surface as well.

Society seems to tell women that we aren't living up to being the ideal woman. In the Christian world, I had always felt that there is an unobtainable goal of being the perfect Christian girl or woman. It was a constant battle of thinking I'm not enough and then came the doubt. I always made myself wonder, why would God love me when I'm not enough?

I sighed as I wondered what words of encouragement I could share with the women in my life who had also expressed these feelings of inadequacy. How could I share anything with them when I was feeling the same way? Wait.

I stopped my car in the middle of the country road. Maybe that was exactly why I should share words of encouragement. We were all on this journey of life, and we were meant to help each other along the way. It was interesting that this theme repeated itself over and over around me. As I continued driving home, I realized I still had more questions and doubts than answers, but I knew I was making progress on this challenging topic.

Chapter 17

AUNT LU GENERALLY TOOK CARE of the grocery shopping in our house. Since she did all the cooking, she knew exactly what she needed and wanted. But her knee had been especially pained recently, so she was not feeling up to walking the store's aisles. I told her I would be happy to go if she provided me with a detailed list of what she needed.

When I parked my car in the grocery store lot, a truck that whipped into a spot near me caught my attention. I sucked in a breath as I saw who it was. I hoped running into Clark like this was a coincidence and that there would not be a confrontation, but my hopes were dashed when he slammed the truck door and came after me as I headed toward the store.

He yelled, "Lydia, stop right there! I want to talk to you!"

I slowly turned to face him, reminding myself to keep calm. "Clark, I don't appreciate your tone of voice, and I don't think this parking lot is the best place for us to have a conversation."

"I'm sick and tired of you telling me what to do and acting better than me. You put my wife up to getting a divorce, and you are going to regret it." He took a step toward me.

"I did not encourage your wife to seek a divorce. That was her decision." I stepped away from him and then resumed my way toward the store.

"We aren't through with this," he threatened. "You were nothing in high school, and you're still nothing, even with your big law degree."

I wasn't going to participate in this conversation, so I kept walking. Clark trailed behind, but the farther I walked, the louder he yelled.

"Everybody knew you were nothing but trash when we were in school. I'm going to make sure the entire town knows that's what you were then and that's what you are now."

I froze in my tracks as Clark stomped back to his truck and got in, slammed the door, and then sped out of the parking lot. Several people were looking at me, and I could tell from their expressions that they were embarrassed to have witnessed this exchange. Groceries were now the last thing on my mind. I needed to go home.

At the farmhouse, I briefly explained to Aunt Lu what had happened. I told her I would go back the next day and shop then. She stood up from her recliner and wrapped me in a hug.

"Honey, you don't have to be so brave and strong. It's okay to cry. It's okay to be sad or angry or any other emotion you are feeling," she reassured me.

"Thank you, Aunt Lu. Right now, I'm in shock. I can't believe he would stoop to harassing me in a parking lot like that. He said some things about me that I don't want to repeat, and I pray that the other people there didn't hear. I think I need to go upstairs and be alone for a little while."

"Of course, dear. I will see you later." She released me from her hug.

My head spun as I trudged up to my bedroom. As was my custom when I was distraught, I pulled my chair to the window. I collapsed into it, but instead of gazing out the window, I put my head in my hands. This was a time to let the tears flow. Tears of anger, confusion, fear, and doubts—they all came out. My conversation with Jordyn about big emotions and then the confrontation with her father filled me. I was nothing but questions and emotions.

The shame and pain from my past also came flooding back stronger than ever. My body shook, and my mind raced from one thought to another. Clark's threat to make sure everyone knew about my past was my worst fear. It was unfolding before my eyes, and I felt powerless to stop or control it. The people in the parking lot probably did hear him, and I wondered how many other people he would tell. Once again, I found myself questioning how God could possibly love me, and I doubted that anyone else could either. How had I ever thought that Sam could love me? My shame was so intense that I didn't feel I could even pray to ask God for help.

Suddenly, I sat up straight in my chair with a realization. This was exactly why I should pray! But what should I say? Where should I begin?

I said out loud, "God, how can you love me?"

I then clearly sensed God lifting me up and holding me and saying, "Because you are my child."

Tears continued to stream down my face as I made my way to my desk. I pulled out my journal to write, but I struggled to find the words to describe everything I was experiencing. Finally, I began.

> *Once again, I find myself revisiting my past traumas. I'm often surprised at how strong the feelings come back. At times, it seems as if I'm repeating the pain, and I'm revisiting each and every bad decision. Shame and guilt come flooding in. I know I cannot change the past, so I'm trying not to dwell on it. I'm trying to remind myself how much I have learned and grown. Though I may flash back to the trauma, I don't have to stay there. I keep telling myself I can leave it behind. God has forgiven me for the chaos that I caused and has cried with me over the trauma I experienced that was not my fault.*
>
> *I know God does not want me to continue living in the past. I also know that God doesn't want me to worry about the future. I cannot spend energy worrying about whether people will learn about my past or worrying about what they might do or say if they find out. God wants me to focus on today. Even when I can't feel His presence, God is with me. God is with me in this moment. And He will be with me in the future as well.*
>
> *Sometimes my past and my inner voices tell me I am not worthy of God's love, but the scriptures tell me the truth. I am a child of God, and I am loved. That voice of shame telling me that I'm not worthy of God's love is lying to me. I must keep reminding myself not to believe these lies. I know all of this, but it is hard to remember it and live it.*

I stopped writing and reviewed what I had written. The pain and voices of my past were difficult to move beyond. I also knew that, with time, I would be able to process all the layers of pain that this confrontation with Clark brought back to the surface. Learning to live in the present moment took time. It was easy to slip back into the habit of lamenting the past and worrying about the future. But there seemed to be a holy peace in being aware of God's presence in this moment, and in the next moment, and the one following that. I knew it would take work to remember that, but learning and growing, like life itself, was a journey and not a destination. I felt a sense of peace that realizing these truths was the first step toward living them.

Chapter 18

IT WAS THE FIRST WEEK OF MAY, which meant it was time for me to speak to Gail's class again, as I had done the previous year. And as I had before, I once again stressed about whether I could share anything interesting with the students or if I would simply bore them. They asked interesting questions after my presentation, which reassured me that I had kept their attention. Though I did not feel called to teach, I enjoyed spending time with these teenagers. It also helped me reconnect with my interest in law. Hearing their interest and excitement about it all rekindled my passion for the subject.

After my presentation, I was thrilled to discover that another teacher, Mr. Carroll, had a free class period. Mr. Carroll had been my favorite English teacher when I was a student at this school. Since I had moved back to the community, I had been able to visit with him a few times. It was at his encouragement that I began journaling. He also had the ability to ask probing questions that always seemed to help me find the answers I was seeking.

I popped into his classroom and found him reading some papers. No doubt, he was grading the never-ending pile of essays he assigned.

"Hello, Mr. Carroll," I said. "I can see that you're busy, but I wanted to stop in and say hello."

He beamed at me as he set the papers he was holding down on the desk in front of him. "Lydia! How nice to see you. These papers can wait. Please, come in and sit for a few minutes. How are you?"

"I just finished talking to one of Gail's classes. I'm always stressed that they will be bored, so I was relieved that they asked questions today. It's always fun to hear their thoughts."

"From what I hear, her students love your presentations. They enjoy people who are passionate about a subject."

I couldn't help but smile. "I was just thinking about how talking to them did rekindle my passion a bit. My energy for my career was waning."

"Oh? Tell me more."

"Truthfully? I've been struggling with some doubts lately. Did I make the correct decision to leave my business and move back here? Why did I decide to hang out a shingle and practice on my own? Why am I here? Etcetera, etcetera."

"Ahh. And I am guessing that having doubts, especially about your career, is not something you are comfortable with. I'm guessing you have always known what you were going to do, planned how to accomplish it, and then completed that plan."

"I'm a type-A personality, you know," I joked.

It was Mr. Carroll's turn to smile. "Oh yes, I'm aware. But there is nothing wrong with doubt, Lydia. It often helps us clarify things—what we believe in, what's important to us. It can either help us change our minds about something or solidify our beliefs. At the very least, doubt is a catalyst for growth."

I nodded in acknowledgment but didn't speak. I was thinking and processing all of this.

Then he continued. "Another possibility is that you are

grieving the end of your old career and the end of your old way of life. Sometimes we can be so caught up in this that we can't discern the new path we are meant to be on. Have you considered the amount of grief you've had to work through? Transition has been a constant theme for you since you decided to move back here."

"I certainly knew I had grief to work through because of my grandmother's death, but you're suggesting I may also have grief because I moved back here?" I raised my eyebrows in surprise. This wasn't something I had thought about.

"My dear, there is no may about it. You left a successful career to move back here and take an unknown path. You had worked extremely hard at a very fast-paced life, and you left that for something very different. In moving back here, you went from a known to a complete unknown. Anytime you change careers and lifestyle as you did, there is some grief involved—and this was not a small change for you. You made a physical move and a major change in both your career and lifestyle."

"I've never considered that view," I said.

"You may be able to quiet some doubts if you ponder this. I'm guessing if you do, then you will have clarity for moving forward. It very well may be the path you are already on, but at least then you will have peace about it."

"I will add this to my list of subjects to write about in my journal."

"Excellent. I love that you're writing. Anytime you would like to share something you've written, I would love to read it."

"At the moment, my writing is simply a way for me to think through things."

"That's the purpose of a great deal of writing. Oh, something else for you to consider—there are stages to grief that you will encounter. As you continue to process your grandmother's death and your career change, you may notice the stages feel different for those two types of griefs. And the pace of these stages may differ as well."

I couldn't think of any response. I had not considered grief as part of my career change. I wondered if I would face all the stages for these separate grief journeys.

I wondered how long I had been sitting, looking out the window and thinking. When I looked back at Mr. Carroll, he was smiling at me, so I'm guessing it had been a while.

I cleared my throat and said, "Well, I should go and let you get back to grading papers."

"Ah, yes. Essays await me."

I stood and made my way toward the door.

"Lydia?" Mr. Carroll said.

I turned around.

"It was so good to see you. And remember, doubt can be the starting place for an amazing adventure."

I smiled again. "Thank you, Mr. Carroll. I will remember that. Thank you for making time for me today."

He waved goodbye, and I left his room. As I walked down the hall, I realized I would need to think about the topics we had discussed. It was amazing that a rather brief conversation could have such deep topics.

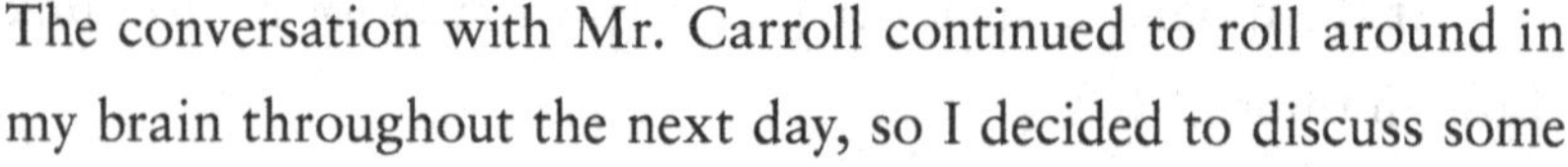

The conversation with Mr. Carroll continued to roll around in my brain throughout the next day, so I decided to discuss some of these ideas with Gail. Since Aunt Lu and I had not entertained guests in a while, I invited her over for dinner. She gladly accepted the opportunity to enjoy Aunt Lu's fabulous cooking. As always, I was an eager assistant, but I simply could not master these recipes. Aunt Lu had told me before that I tried too hard. She said I needed to relax and enjoy the process of cooking. For some reason, the thought of trying too hard struck me. I wondered if a person could try too hard in other areas of life as well.

After we had filled ourselves with pot roast, potatoes, carrots, and the best triple-berry pie I had ever eaten, Gail and I poured some glasses of wine and went to sit on the porch. It was a beautiful evening. The breeze was exactly what was needed to keep the temperature perfect.

Gail jumped right into a conversation. "Once again, my students are raving about you."

I blushed a bit and asked, "Why?"

"It's your passion for law, your experience in government, and your knowledge of the constitution. Instead of just being words on a page, you make this information come alive."

"I must confess, speaking to them and seeing their interest has helped me too. As you know, I've been having doubts about moving back here, and I've even been wondering if I should explore completely different career options. I realized I was just going through the motions with my practice. But talking to your class showed me I'm still passionate about it. I'll continue my little practice for now, but I'm also going to spend time volunteering with the domestic violence and sexual assault support center."

Gail grinned from ear to ear. "Oh, that makes me so happy. I'm glad this experience was as positive for you as it was for my class and me. Now, tell me about where you are with your doubts."

"I had an interesting conversation with Mr. Carroll after I spoke to your class," I said.

"He's a fascinating man with exceptional wisdom. I would love to hear about your conversation."

"He wondered if part of what I called doubt was actually grief, particularly surrounding my old career and way of life. He said that at times, we can be caught up in grief and not be able to discern the path we should be on."

Gail nodded. "That makes sense. Leaving your career behind and beginning a completely new life could create changes that need to be processed. I can see how those changes could lead to grief. Do you think this is true for you?"

"It's something I'm thinking about."

"Did he have any other wisdom about doubts?"

"Just that pursuing our doubts can often be a catalyst for growth."

Gail nodded again. "What do you think about that concept?"

I smiled. "I think I have plenty of things to think about."

Gail laughed. "It certainly sounds like it!"

"I've always thought that doubt was bad and that I should be ashamed of it. It seemed like a weakness or something. But now? After listening to you and Mr. Carroll, I guess I feel like I've been given permission to have doubts. I need to give these ideas some serious consideration."

Gail paused for a moment and then said, "If you follow these questions you're having, you might decide to modify or completely change some of the decisions you've made. Or you may learn with certainty that your decisions were the correct ones for you.

I hope this doesn't sound condescending, but I'm proud of you for wanting to grow and for not dismissing these suggestions. I know it is challenging to lean into all of this."

"Thanks, Gail. That's not condescending at all. I've been on a growing journey, and I will continue that. I also know it's going to take time to process whatever grief I'm experiencing from my career change. And Mr. Carroll reminded me that the grief I process from Grandmother's death may look and feel different from that of my career change. So, I guess that means I still have work to do."

"I think you might be correct, and I'm guessing you may fill up your writing journal."

Gail sat for another minute, gazing into her wine glass. "We've talked about some deep topics this evening."

"Yes, we have," I agreed.

"Let's both do some thinking and discuss these again sometime. But now the time has come for me to get going because I must teach tomorrow."

After we said goodbye and Gail left, I went back to my chair on the porch. I wanted to enjoy the beautiful breeze a little longer. Besides, I had too much on my mind to sleep anytime soon.

Chapter 19

My conversation with Gail from the previous night was the first thing on my mind when I woke up the next morning. Since I'd moved back home, my life had been filled with deep, soul thinking. Spiritual transformation was difficult and time-consuming. I thought it might be even more challenging than all my years in school, but I knew it was worth the effort.

I glanced at the clock and realized I should stop thinking for the time being and get moving instead. I thought of myself as an early riser, but I rarely woke earlier than Aunt Lu. When I went downstairs, I found her in the middle of baking a pie.

"That smells delicious! Are we having pie for breakfast?"

"I'm sorry, Lydia, but this one goes to Reverend Peters. His birthday is tomorrow, and I wanted to do something special for him," Aunt Lu said.

"I'm sure he will love it. Both the pie and the thought behind it."

"Are you running any errands today, dear? I thought you might be willing to take it to him."

"I'd be happy to do that. Do we have any birthday cards around here? I'm not going to bake a pie, but I would love to write him a short note."

"I'm sure we do. And I'm guessing he will enjoy a note from you as much as this pie."

I smiled at Aunt Lu. I couldn't imagine anyone would equate a note with one of her pies, but I wanted to give him my thanks and appreciation for the various ways he served and loved our congregation.

Later that morning, I drove to the church. It occurred to me on the way that I should have confirmed if Reverend Peters was in his office, but I decided to continue anyway. I was pleased when I saw his car in the parking lot, and I found him in his office, reading.

"Hello, Reverend Peters. May I interrupt?"

"Hi, Lydia. Please, come in. It's so good to see you."

I held out the pie box. "I have a pie from Aunt Lu and a card from both of us. Happy birthday a day early."

"Aren't you and Lu kind to remember. I know my family and I will enjoy this treat with our celebration. Please, sit down. It's been on my mind to call you again to see if your small group is still going well."

"It is. We have a great group, both in numbers and participation. Of course, not everyone can attend every week, but the attendance has been very consistent especially considering how busy these women are."

"That's wonderful! I'm so glad your group has become a true community for you all. Have there been any concerns raised or topics you've discussed that you need guidance with?"

I decided I would wait to discuss the idea of being enough until another day because I wanted to try to further clarify my own thoughts about it first. Instead, I decided to ask a question that had been on my mind for a long time. "There is something I've been wanting to ask you. It hasn't been discussed by our group, but it's something on my mind. How do you know if the voice that you are hearing is truly God?"

"Do you suppose we could start with a warm-up question?" Reverend Peters smile always put me at ease. "That can be a difficult one. It takes discernment to differentiate between the voices we hear. Not long ago, I read something by Teresa of Avila. She was a nun who lived in the 1500s. I like what she said. She had three clues that would help you know if the voice you heard was God's. The first is in the power and authority of the voice you are hearing. She further described it as something is better because of what you heard. The second clue is the peace you feel in your soul, and the third is that the words stick in your memory better than a typical conversation. I like those tests. Even though she lived hundreds of years ago, I think it is still good wisdom."

"I agree. I've felt the peace that she mentioned. There was also a time when I felt excitement but also fear at the same time," I said.

Reverend Peters laughed heartily. "That was definitely God. Exciting and scary is an excellent description of a message from God. Do you mind if I ask what it was regarding?"

"It was about leaving my career and moving back here."

He nodded in acknowledgment. "I wondered if your decision was based on a call from God, and now I know without a doubt that it was. It sounds to me like God was calling you to a new purpose."

"Absolutely. It wasn't long after Grandmother's death when this happened, and I was trying to decide what was next for me. I heard God telling me my career had been based on my motives and desires and not on my true purpose. Most of my former clients were rather impersonal, and they simply needed me for greedy intentions. I came to view my career as shallow and without true purpose."

"That is powerful. You certainly have had experience hearing and following God's voice. Since I quoted a sixteenth century nun, let me quote a saint from the early thirteenth century. St. Francis of Assisi said, 'Satan will try to turn our minds and hearts away from God by making us think we can have or do something more valuable.'

"You told Satan something the day you made the decision to leave your career. You knew and acted on the fact that we cannot have or do anything that is better than following God's will. My preacher friends like to say, 'That will preach.' Anytime you would like to share this message with the congregation, let me know."

I'm sure I was blushing when I replied, "Oh, Reverend, I'm still just trying to comprehend exactly what God is calling me to do."

"We all are. For our entire lives. It seems to me you are doing a wonderful job of discerning God's purpose for you."

"Thank you, Reverend Peters. I'm trying," I said. "Well, I better let you get back to work. I have some projects awaiting me as well."

"Take care, Lydia. And please come back so we can talk again."

"I will do that."

As I drove back to the farm, I thought about the quotes Reverend Peters shared. I thought I might want to research Teresa of Avila and St. Francis. What Reverend Peters had shared illustrated that wisdom can transcend the years. They seemed to offer ample ideas to contemplate even though they had lived centuries earlier. I had enjoyed my conversation with Reverend Peters, and I decided that the next time I visited, I would prepare some questions so I could continue to pick his brain for wisdom.

Sam pulled up to the farmhouse right ahead of me. He parked by the shed and started walking toward the garage. I was glad to see him because I wanted to talk to him about Ellie, but we had not had a chance to visit for a while. As he approached, I noticed a strange look on his face. He looked very anxious, and that was not typical for him.

"Hi, Sam. What are you up to today?"

"I need to talk to you about something. I stopped by a bit ago, but Lu said you took a pie to Reverend Peters. She didn't think you would be too long."

"And I wouldn't have been gone very long, but we got to talking."

Sam nodded. I'm sure he wasn't surprised that the two of us could get caught up discussing life. "Well, I need someone to talk to, and you're the person I keep thinking of."

"Sure. What's up?"

"Can we walk around while we talk? This is hard, and I need to keep moving."

"Absolutely." I swallowed hard. I didn't know why, but I was nervous about what could be so hard to talk about.

We wandered around the farm for a while, but Sam didn't say anything. I came close a couple of times to saying, "Just say it!" but I knew it was best to wait until he was ready to talk. Eventually, he stopped and stared at the ground. He finally said,

"I'm still concerned about Ellie. She seems so depressed. I don't mean that she's going to hurt herself, but she's just not herself."

"She's going through a major change in her life. I'm not surprised she doesn't seem like herself," I told him gently.

"I know, but this is . . . I don't know . . . it's hard to describe. That's why I'm struggling to know what to say. Maybe it's nothing. It's more of a gut feeling."

"Can you give me any examples?"

He thought for a moment and then said, "Well, here's one. The other night, she was cooking dinner and the recipe didn't go quite right, and she just sobbed about it. I've never seen her cry like that."

"Do you think she could have been crying about something else and not dinner?"

Sam looked up at me. "Do you think that's it? She was crying about something different than what it appeared to be?"

"It could be. The dinner could be like the proverbial straw that broke the camel's back. It's just another disappointment. One more example of 'I can't do anything right.' The pain and trauma keep accumulating, and then the thing that causes you to lose it isn't what you're actually upset about at all."

"Wow. It sounds like this has happened to you," he said.

My breath caught in my chest. Had I really just blurted all of that out? I didn't usually share such personal feelings, and I was especially embarrassed to share them with Sam. I didn't want to reveal my pain to him. I tried to recover by saying, "I think many people do this. Or at least many women do. I don't know if men do it as well because I don't typically have that type of conversation with men."

Sam nodded. He seemed to understand.

"I hope this isn't too personal, but how are you doing with all of this? I mean, you have two roommates in a house that isn't big. And they're going through an exceedingly difficult time. It would be understandable if you are feeling some stress as well," I said.

Sam bowed his head, stuffed his hands deep into his pockets, and started walking again. I caught up and walked beside him. A few minutes passed before he stopped again and looked me straight in the eyes.

"One of the reasons I decided to talk to you is because I know you can keep a confidence. I don't want you to say anything to anyone because I don't want this getting back to Ellie. I'm afraid it might hurt her feelings, but if I'm honest, I'm feeling a little overwhelmed. I want to help her, but I don't know how. I've tried a couple of times, and she acted like she doesn't want help. But then the next day she cried because dinner didn't go as planned. I just don't know what to do or if there's even anything I can do."

"That sounds like a tough place to be. I'm sorry you are all going through this. It's hard."

"That's not the worst of what I'm feeling." Sam dropped his head even further. I didn't know what to do. I wanted to reach out and touch him, but I guarded my actions. I was shocked at my deep reaction to his show of emotion.

I finally asked, "Do you want to talk about it?"

He looked up, and the expression on his face was foreign to me. This was not like the Sam I knew. Instead of a face full of peace, I saw anguish. "I'm angry at God, Lydia. Angry and let down. And scared. I mean, it's not right to feel this way about God."

"Can you tell me more about the letdown part?"

"You know—disappointed. Why did God let this happen? Where is He in all of this? I try not to think about it because I don't think I should feel this way toward God, but then these feelings just keep coming back." He looked away as if the shame he was experiencing about his emotions was too profound to show me.

I couldn't stop myself this time. I reached out and gently touched his arm. "Sam, God is big enough to handle all your emotions," I told him. "I know this because He's told me so. You've been through an ordeal, and values that you hold very dear have been broken. I think it's only natural to wonder where God is in all this pain. I don't think it's wrong to feel as you do, but I do think you need to work through these emotions. You can't stay stuck here for long or it will weigh on you heavily."

In a strained voice, he asked, "How do I work through it?"

"I don't think you will be able to do it on your own. Perhaps you could talk to Reverend Peters. I find him easy to talk to."

Sam nodded. "Yeah, he is. Maybe I'll do that."

"I think you'll find that you will feel better if you can talk this through with someone. It also occurs to me that I haven't invited Ellie to our small group. It might help her to have a group of women to connect with. I'll call and invite her."

"Thanks, Lydia. She can use all the support she can get. And thanks for listening. I appreciate not only your listening skills, but also your wisdom." He smiled, and it was as if the old Sam was standing in front of me again. There was a look of some peace in his eyes.

Now it was my turn to look away. I couldn't look him in the eye because I was afraid he would see my growing feelings for him. "You're welcome. I'm happy to help." Then I decided to change the subject before I revealed anything else.

"Would you like some lemonade or maybe something to eat?"

"That sounds great," he said.

We walked back to the house in silence. It seemed we were each deep in our own thoughts.

Chapter 20

I KEPT MY WORD AND INVITED ELLIE to our next small group meeting. She gave me various excuses for why she couldn't come, including that she was too tired after working all day, she needed to spend time with Jordyn, and she wasn't ready to be out in a group yet. I told her that I understood her fear, but I had learned that the thing I didn't want to do or make time for was often the very thing I needed the most. I told her I thought she could use a supportive community with other women. Plus, she needed some time for herself. She finally agreed she would come once and see what she thought about it.

When it came time for our meeting, I waited for Ellie in the parking lot. We had a full crowd, and I was thrilled to see Anna and Sarah. I knew that if they talked about their recent struggles, then Ellie would know she wasn't alone. Gail and I had planned what questions to lead off with after our usual sharing time, but those flew out the window when Ellie immediately shared that she was concerned about her daughter.

"I know this is my first time here, and I don't know what's come over me, but I just need to get this out. My daughter confided to me the other night that she feels invisible. She says she thinks she's a nobody. We cried together, and I did my best to console her. But honestly, life has been so hard for me lately that I'm not sure I'm in a good place to help her."

As usual, the other women all jumped in with support. Their consensus was that parenting is often a challenging job, but when you are going through difficulties yourself, it's even harder.

Anna brought the topic back to Ellie's concern when she said, "Let's talk about the issue of feeling invisible. I'm an adult, and I've felt that way myself. Does anybody else ever feel like that?"

Around the room, I saw several women nod in agreement. It appeared that several of us had also experienced this feeling. I glanced at Sarah and noticed her gaze was fixed on her shoes. I silently prayed that this conversation was not too difficult for her. Then, to my surprise, she jumped into the conversation.

"I've been feeling invisible and worthless myself. I haven't talked about it, but I was fired from my job recently. Not only am I scared, but I feel lost. And invisible," she shared.

Several women spoke at once. "Oh honey, I thought you didn't seem like yourself lately," one woman said. "I'm so sorry you're going through this," someone else mentioned. "That's awful, Sarah. Is there anything we can do?" a third woman asked.

Seemingly overwhelmed by their kindness and support, Sarah started to sob. If she was anything like me, I knew this was a good sign. I had learned in my own life that you cannot keep your emotions squashed down. Gail stood and walked over to Sarah's chair, asking if she could give her a hug. Sarah nodded.

As the two hugged each other, many in the room also seemed to be overwhelmed with emotion. Our hearts ached for those who had shared their pain that day, and I'm sure we each thought of our own pains as well.

Finally, Gail went back to her chair and bowed her head

for a minute. Then she looked up at us and said, "Friends, I'm so thankful for this group. I'm so grateful we have built this community where we feel safe enough to share what we're going through. And I'm thankful for the wisdom and support we share with each other. We respond to each other with love. I appreciate each of you, and your willingness to share the hard parts of life."

There was a great deal of sniffing and blowing of noses happening around the room now. There didn't seem to be a dry eye anywhere.

After a minute or two of quiet reflection, Ellie spoke again. "I'm hesitant to share this, but I feel that I need to be honest with all of you. I've been doubting my faith lately. I go back and forth between being angry at God and questioning if I even believe in God anymore. It seems wrong to say this in a church, but it's the truth about where I am right now."

A look of compassion came upon Gail's face as she heard the pain in Ellie's voice. "Oh, Ellie, I hear your pain and anger. I want you to know it's okay to have those feelings and doubts." She turned her attention to the whole group. "Some of you have heard me say this before, but I once read a quote that said, 'Doubt is not a sin. It can be a launching point toward deep faith.' What we've been taught about anger and doubting our faith, well . . . I think it's all lies. A doubt is a desire and a need for more. More time. More experiences for faith to speak to us.

"Doubt and anger do not mean you aren't a Christian. They certainly don't mean that God is going to come after you. We shouldn't be upset or ashamed if we or someone we love has doubt because, as that quote stated, doubt can be a launching point toward deep faith. We also shouldn't be ashamed of our feelings. Instead, we should pursue where they will lead us. Doing this often helps people mature in their faith. When I've taken my doubts and questions to God, I have received loving answers or at least loving assurances."

Gail paused for a moment and then smiled. "I'm sorry, friends. I guess I'm passionate about this topic. From what I've shared, you can probably guess that I've had my own questions over the years. Does anyone have a response to all of this? Or questions?"

Anna jumped back into the conversation. "All I can say is thank you. Thank you for your thoughts on doubt and everything we have discussed in this group. I've learned so much about faith and about myself since we started this group." Emotion filled her voice, and she was barely able to speak, but we heard her say, "You all mean the world to me, and I'm so thankful for you."

It had been an emotional evening. We sat in this space of quiet, each of us deep in our own thoughts and perhaps in our own problems and pain. After a few minutes, Gail asked us to join hands and pray. We stood and came together in a circle.

"Gracious and loving God," she began, "thank you for being in this room with your children. We are each so thankful for this group of caring friends. Some of us have been through difficult times. We ask that you continue to be with each of us on our journeys. Thank you for your patience as we come to you with our doubts and questions, and even our strong emotions. Thank you for sending the Holy Spirit, which we feel as the peace that surpasses all understanding. Fill us to overflowing with that peace and with your love. And now, God, as the time has come for each of us to go our individual ways, bless us in the coming days. In Jesus's name, amen."

Because we were the facilitators of the group, Gail and I always stayed until everyone else had gone. The others usually left soon after the meeting concluded. This time, however, almost everyone wanted to linger and chat in smaller groups. When Gail and I were finally alone, I sat down again. Gail joined me.

"Are you okay?" she asked.

"That was . . . I don't even know how to describe what that was. Painful, perhaps? I'm sensing pain coming at me from multiple directions."

"Yes, there was definitely pain tonight. But there was something else too."

"What?"

"I felt the presence of God in this room. And I felt His peace."

I slowly looked up at Gail, and I didn't try to hide the emotions I was feeling. "I guess since I'm still struggling with what we heard tonight, I felt the pain and not the peace."

"You know it's okay to still be searching, right? It's okay not to have all the answers," Gail said.

I shrugged. "I still feel like something is missing. I'm still searching for something, but I don't know what. I rediscovered my faith, so I don't know what could be missing. Maybe I shouldn't be co-leading this group with you."

"Lydia, we are all still searching and growing. If you're open to growing and learning, then you are in the right place. If it's your doubts you're concerned about, don't be. Lean into God with your pain. One thing I didn't say tonight that I should have is this—a faith without questions is stalled, or a nongrowing faith.

Questions encourage us to continue growing and learning." She paused and looked straight into my eyes. "I haven't mentioned this to you before, but I need to say it now. You experienced significant trauma in your life—truthfully, numerous significant traumas. And they happened years before you acknowledged them. It takes time to fully face that. There are many layers to peel back, and you can't heal them all at once. You must revisit these traumas so you can keep healing the layers, and that takes time. I know this is hard to hear, but you are a dear friend, and I want you to continue on your road to recovery."

I sighed deeply. "Deep down, I know you're right. I'm still bothered by my former partner's phone call, and Ellie's situation is never far from my thoughts. And I still don't want to even consider a relationship with Sam or anyone else. You once told me you thought I should work on myself before I entered a relationship, and that was some of the best advice I've ever heard. Since I still don't feel comfortable even considering a relationship, I think that is my soul telling me I still have healing to do."

Gail nodded and said, "That might be, but there's also another possibility. Are you afraid of a relationship? Are you afraid of being hurt again and the pain that would come with that hurt?"

I almost jumped up from my chair and with a defensive tone in my voice, I said, "Who wouldn't be afraid? When you've only experienced pain in relationships, it makes you believe that's how all relationships end!" I took a deep breath to calm myself down. "I'm sorry I snapped, Gail. I guess my response proves that I am afraid. I also don't want to harm the good relationship I have with Sam."

Gail patted my knee. "It's okay, friend. I understand. I think this might go beyond the trauma. Fear is what's left behind. You will need to dig deep and take risks as you explore these fears. In fact, if you haven't seen your therapist recently, perhaps you should schedule an appointment to discuss this. I don't think you can process this on your own."

I knew she was correct. I needed to dig deeper and face this fear, and I would need help to do it.

"Since we're sharing, there's something else I haven't told you. Clark confronted me in the grocery store parking lot a few days ago. He kept yelling that I encouraged Ellie to get a divorce. And then, in front of everybody, he said that I was trash in high school, and that he was going to be sure the entire town knew it. This is my worst fear, people knowing about my past. Shame is ruling my thoughts, and I'm back to wondering how God could love me."

"Oh, Lydia, I am so sorry. That must be terribly painful. But you know deep in your soul that God does love you, and you need to keep asking Him for guidance. You are more than these traumas you've faced. They are a part of you, but they're not the end of your story."

She stopped talking and just looked at me. Then she said, "You're going to be good, my friend. I can see it in your eyes. Those aren't the eyes to a closed-off soul. Those are the eyes to a soul that is yearning to grow in her knowledge of and relationship with God. A woman who knows deep in her soul that she is loved."

We sat quietly in our own thoughts for several minutes. Eventually, Gail patted my knee again and said, "We could probably sit here all night, reflecting and talking, but it's a school night for me. Are you okay if we lock up and head home?"

I smiled. "It's not a school night for me, but I'm exhausted. Let's close the door on this meeting."

Chapter 21

THE DEPTH OF THE CONVERSATIONS raised at our meeting and afterward with Gail kept me awake most of the night. Her comments about having layers of trauma to work through particularly replayed in my mind. I knew she was right, but I was torn about how to proceed. How do you lean in further when you think you've already explored your trauma? How do you address all these layers? I also knew she was right about my fear of relationships. It was crippling. I was glad I had an appointment with my therapist already scheduled because I knew I needed help to address these questions.

When sleep wouldn't come, I decided to get up. It was one of the rare mornings when I was awake before Aunt Lu. I made some coffee and went to sit on the porch. I was still there mulling everything over when Aunt Lu woke up. She must have sensed something was wrong, but she didn't ask about it. Instead, she brought a piece of coffee cake and a small bowl of fresh fruit and set them on the table beside me, and then she went back inside without saying a word.

I was still deep in thought when I finally realized that Mrs. Dalton was standing in front of me.

"Mrs. Dalton, I'm so sorry. Have you been here long? I didn't hear you."

"I'm not surprised. You were sitting there so still that for a minute I thought you had gone and left us. Are you okay?"

"Oh, yes, I was just deep in thought."

"Honey, if you go any deeper, you aren't going to be able to climb back out. This will make you come to life, though. I brought you and Lu fresh strawberries. I cut some up last night and put it over ice cream. Might be the best strawberries I've ever grown. Or maybe I say that about fresh strawberries every year."

"I agree with you Mrs. Dalton. I love fresh strawberries. Would you like to sit and have some coffee? I would love to return the favor of your hospitality and treat you for a change."

"That would be nice, Lydia," she said.

"Would you like to sit out here on the porch, or would you rather go inside?"

"I think the porch would be lovely. Let me take these strawberries inside and talk to Lu. Then I will be right back."

"I can take them inside and grab some coffee for you."

"No, I want to talk to Lu. I need to tell her that you and I have some private business to discuss."

Before I could say anything else, she was in the house. Private business to discuss? What private business would Mrs. Dalton want to discuss with me? I didn't have to wait long to find out because she came right back outside with coffee and a piece of coffee cake.

"Lu told me she already brought you a piece. I hope you don't mind if I sit here and enjoy this while we talk," she said, sitting in the chair beside me.

"Not at all. I must confess, I'm curious what private business we need to discuss," I said.

"Well, it's not business in the way you're thinking. It's me getting into your business. From the look on your face, it appears you're still not back to yourself after we talked the last time. Are you still wondering if you're enough?"

Talk about getting right to the point. I was so surprised by her directness that I almost fell out of my chair. There was no side stepping a topic with Mrs. Dalton, so I decided to be as honest as I could.

"I've been talking to several women lately, and this topic just keeps coming up. One woman's husband was unfaithful, so she's wondering why she wasn't enough for him. One woman's children are now all grown. Without having them at home, she wonders if she's enough without that role to fill. One woman was fired from her job, and she wonders the same. I left my previous career, and I'm still not positive about what's next, so yes, I'm still wondering if I'm enough. Even after our talk, I guess I'm still doubting."

"It sounds like you are. And those other folks are just adding fuel to your own doubts. I know you are big into reading to learn something, and there's only one book that's going to help you with this topic. That's the Bible. But just reading it isn't going to be enough. You are going to need to feel and *know* this knowledge. You won't ever feel that you are enough if you only look to a job, your appearance, a man, or a role to fulfill you. That's not what this is about. It's not even about what size clothes you wear, how much money you have, or what important job you have. None of that. Feeling that you are enough needs to come from understanding that you are made by God and loved by God. Get out your Bible and carefully read the first book, Genesis. It says you are enough."

"It does?"

"Yes, child, it does. I told you before that you are a child of

God. In Genesis, it says that God made you in His image. You are made in the image of God! So, if God's enough, and I sure hope you think so, then you are enough."

She'd knocked me for a loop again. I had never thought about how being made in God's image meant I was enough.

It seemed that Mrs. Dalton wasn't done preaching yet. "I've had plenty of struggles in my life. When my husband died years ago, I had to face a lot of problems. Was I going to run a farm by myself, or was I going to sell what had been in my family for years? Folks were shocked when I didn't sell and decided to work it on my own. Of course, I had help now and again, but mostly it's been me. There were a few times when I looked in the mirror and wondered what this scrawny woman was doing.

"One day I heard Him—I'm talking God here. I heard Him say I could do it. He said, 'You are enough just as you are, just as I made you, and you can do this work.' That's when I knew I was enough. God told me I was, just as I am. You need to hear this from God too. And so do those other ladies."

We were quiet for a moment, and then she spoke again. "My, I've shared a sermon this morning! And I let my coffee get cold while I did all that talking. Have I left you with something to think about?"

"Yes, ma'am, you have," I assured her.

"Good. Now, get to thinking about it. I'm going to go get a warmed up cup of coffee, and then we will talk about something else. How would that be?"

"That would be good."

I smiled as she went back into the house. She had most definitely given me something to think about. I loved how I was surrounded by wisdom. Though I realized I would always miss my grandmother, I remembered all her words of wisdom to me. And now I had Gail and Mrs. Dalton and Mr. Carroll and countless others. One who is surrounded by loving wisdom is a blessed person. I was still smiling when Mrs. Dalton came back out.

"Well, I see you are already smiling. That is a good sign," she said.

"I was just thinking about how blessed I am to have so many wise friends. Thank you for sharing with me."

"You're welcome, honey. I do want you to keep thinking about all of this, but then you will need to share the wisdom with others."

"I will. I promise."

She smiled and then said, "Now, on to other important matters. Did you plant anything new and exciting in your garden this year?"

I didn't want to laugh for fear of offending her, but I loved how we moved so quickly from a serious conversation on theology to discussing the garden. But to Mrs. Dalton, they were equally important. Perhaps that in itself was an important lesson. We discussed gardens and crops and other topics as well. Finally, Mrs. Dalton looked at her watch and told me she had loafed around for half the day and that she had chores to do. With that, she left. I decided I needed to follow her example and get to work as well.

Chapter 22

MRS. DALTON DIDN'T SIMPLY bring enough strawberries to enjoy with a scoop of ice cream. She was so generous in her sharing that we decided to freeze most of what she'd brought. Aunt Lu thought it would be fun if I invited Gail over to help us. I'm not sure that freezing strawberries would be my definition of fun, but I knew it would be nice to have help. Gail was delighted to be invited.

Of course, as usual, Aunt Lu thought we needed nourishment before we began our task. She had tried a new scone recipe, and we were delighted to give her our rave reviews. We then began to wash and slice what seemed like a never-ending pile of strawberries.

"What will you do with all of these strawberries?" Gail asked.

Aunt Lu answered, "Well, we will freeze some of them."

Gail smiled. "I meant what will you use them for? Surely you and Lydia can't eat them all."

"Oh, heavens no. I will use some of them to make pies for various functions. Then, I suspect we will pull some out of the freezer to enjoy in the middle of winter. Nothing brightens a cold winter day like homegrown strawberries. And I also think I will use some of them to make preserves. Lydia, you like strawberry preserves, don't you?"

"It's one of my favorites," I replied. Then, turning to Gail,

I said, "Now you know the secret. People give Aunt Lu extra produce, and she turns it into something delicious and gives it back to them. I'm sure something yummy will be coming your way."

Aunt Lu confirmed my suspicions. "Indeed, Gail. I thought I would send you home with a strawberry pie or two to share with the other teachers."

Gail shrieked with excitement. "That would be wonderful! Mr. Carroll often remarks about your wonderful pies."

Aunt Lu beamed. She was glad to bring joy to others through her cooking.

Gail then said, "Lydia, I almost forgot. I need to take my car to the dealer for some work. It's nothing major, but it will take long enough that I can't wait. Would you have any time this week to meet me there and then take me to school?"

"I'd be happy to. Just let me know the day."

It took us most of the afternoon to wash and prepare the strawberries. While Gail and I sliced them, Aunt Lu used some to make a couple of pies. This pie recipe, she explained, didn't have a traditional crust. Instead, it was like a shortbread cookie recipe. Gail watched carefully and asked questions about the recipe itself and about Aunt Lu's techniques.

I remarked, "Aunt Lu, I think you should teach some cooking classes. You could probably use the kitchen at the church."

Gail loved the idea and enthusiastically added, "I will be the first to sign up. I cook well enough to feed myself, but you amaze me, Lu."

Aunt Lu blushed. "You girls are too much. People might enjoy eating my cooking, but they don't want me teaching them how to do it."

"Oh, I think people would enjoy it," Gail told her.

"I'll think about it. But right now, we've got enough work here with these strawberries."

She was correct. When we were finished, I was exhausted and enjoyed an evening of relaxing with my feet propped up.

It took a few days for Gail to schedule her car repairs. On the day of the appointment, I met her at the dealership and then drove her to school. I noticed that Mr. Carroll's car was there when we pulled into the school parking lot, and I asked Gail if she thought it would be okay to stop in and say hello to him. She was confident Mr. Carroll would enjoy my visit.

When I reached his classroom, I stuck my head through the doorway and asked if he had a few minutes.

"Why, Lydia, what brings you here at this early hour?" he asked.

"Gail needed a ride, so I volunteered. I don't want to interrupt if you are in the middle of something."

"A teacher's work is never done, but this can wait while we visit for a bit. How are you?"

"I'm just going to jump right in and say that I'm still confused," I said.

"Go on."

"I've had multiple conversations recently where the subject of not being enough has arisen."

Mr. Carroll nodded silently, so I continued. "The situation for each of them is different, but this doubt or feeling is the same.

They each say they're not enough or that they're not worthy." I gazed out the window.

"How have you responded to these women?" he prompted.

I continued to gaze out the window, wondering why I was talking to Mr. Carroll about this. But since I'd started, I felt I should continue. I faced him again and admitted, "I haven't truly responded to them yet. Or at least, I haven't had words of wisdom for them."

"Why is that? You are a wise woman."

"I don't think so. I think I'm struggling more than they are."

"Where is it written that wise women don't have struggles? That is where wisdom often arises. Have you struggled with feelings of worth?" he asked.

I looked out the window again. "I think you should change the past tense of your question to the present tense." I glanced at Mr. Carroll to see a small smile.

"I see," he said.

"I also had an interesting conversation with Vera Dalton. Do you know her?"

"Her name is not familiar. What was this conversation about?"

"She said that being enough is not about jobs or relationships or anything like that. She also said I should read the book of Genesis because that's where God says I'm enough because He made me in His image."

"Ah, indeed, it does say that. I think she has provided you with excellent wisdom."

"Do you think so? I mean, that sounds too easy—you're enough because you are made in God's image. So, why don't we all know that we're enough?"

"Because it is not easy. Part of the problem is that advertisers and society as a whole don't want us to believe that we are enough on our own. They want us to purchase the next best thing to make us feel whole and to keep the economy growing. But truthfully, it's even deeper and older than that. Satan has been using this same lie since Genesis. That's what he told Eve, 'You are not enough, but you will be enough when you have this apple.' Satan told her that God was withholding things from her and that she would never be all she could be because God was holding something back. If she would simply take the apple, then she would be complete. Who wants to be inferior? Eve doubted herself, and Satan provided lies."

"I guess we all know how that played out for Adam and Eve," I said.

"Exactly. I think what Vera Dalton told you and what I am telling you now is, do not believe Satan's lies. We are all made in God's image, so He made us to be enough. He is not withholding from us. All we need to do is find our way back to Him."

I sensed there was wisdom in this message. Then the bell rang to begin the school day, so I thanked Mr. Carroll for his time and made my way to the door.

"Lydia," Mr. Carroll called out to me. I turned around to face him again. "You are enough. In fact, I would say that you are an extraordinary woman of God."

I couldn't speak. I placed my hand over my heart to indicate that I had not only heard but felt his assurance.

Chapter 23

THE LEADERSHIP TEAM AT CHURCH scheduled an evening of fun activities for the congregation. The event included a potluck dinner, a time for singing, and a time for board games. Aunt Lu insisted that we go. Even though I was exhausted, I didn't want to disappoint her. Besides, Aunt Lu had baked some wonderful looking pies, and the only way I would enjoy a piece was if I attended.

All of the food was amazing. Several people went from table to table in search of the baker who had contributed an amazing chocolate pecan pie. Of course, that person was Aunt Lu. There were other delicious contributions to the potluck as well, and over the course of the evening, I heard many promises around the room to share recipes. Sam sat next to me and inquired as to what incredible dish I had made. I was embarrassed when I confessed that I had made nothing, but I recovered by assuring him that I did most of the cleanup and carried all of Aunt Lu's contributions inside for her.

When most people had finished eating, Reverend Peters asked Janelle, our church pianist, and Margaret, who led our singing every Sunday, to lead us in a few hymns. As our time of singing seemed to be ending, Margaret asked me to come over. I pretended not to hear her, but Sam insisted I go. When I reached her, she said she wanted our last hymn of the evening to be "It Is Well With My Soul." Margaret and I had sung this song at the luncheon after my grandmother's funeral. It had been one of Grandmother's favorites.

The hymn also reminded me of the question my grandmother had asked me not long before she died. Her question, *how is it with your soul?* had sent me searching. After her death, I spent a great deal of time praying and soul searching before I could answer that it really was well.

I hoped I could remember all the words and that I could sing it without sobbing.

> *When peace, like a river, attendeth my way,*
> *When sorrows like sea billows roll;*
> *Whatever my lot, thou hast taught me to say,*
> *It is well, it is well with my soul.*

> *It is well, with my soul,*
> *It is well, it is well with my soul*

> *My sin, oh, the bliss of this glorious thought!*
> *My sin, not in part but the whole,*
> *Is nailed to the cross, and I bear it no more,*
> *Praise the Lord, praise the Lord, O my soul!*

This time on the chorus, I echoed Margaret.

> *It is well, it is well, with my soul, with my soul.*
> *It is well, it is well with my soul.*

As we ended the chorus, Margaret whispered that I should take the lead on the last verse. It was too late to argue, so I let my deep alto voice ring out.

And, Lord, haste the day when my faith shall be sight,
The clouds be rolled back like a scroll;
The trumpet shall sound, and the Lord shall descend,
Praise the Lord, praise the Lord, oh my soul.

It is well, it is well, with my soul, with my soul,
It is well, it is well with my soul.

Reverend Peters came over and thanked us. As I walked back to my seat, he announced that after we had cleared the tables, we would begin the board games. Sam smiled when I sat down.

"That was wonderful. I enjoy listening to you sing," he said.

I blushed for the second time, but I managed to say thank you. Then I stood, gathered the dishes around me, and took them to the kitchen. I volunteered for kitchen duty partly because I didn't want to play games, but more important, I felt awkward being around Sam. I had continued ignoring my feelings for him and had convinced myself I still wasn't ready for a relationship. Fear still surged through me anytime I thought about being in one.

When I finished cleaning up, Gail pulled me into the hallway. "I've been praying about our conversation about being enough and still having healing to work through," she said. "Another idea occurred to me. I'm wondering if you need to share with other people about your traumas before you can experience deeper healing. When trauma is a secret, it's difficult to heal. It's as if it's holding you hostage. So to heal, you need to get the secret out of the private world."

I looked around to make sure no one else was in the hall. "Are you joking? Who do you suggest I tell? It's not something you just bring up in casual conversation."

"What about our small group? They are all caring women."

I paused. Something deep inside said that was a bad idea, but I wasn't sure if that was just fear of not wanting the truth to be told or if there was another reason for what I was feeling. I decided to be honest with Gail.

"Look, for some reason I don't think I want to discuss it with the group. I'll think about this, but I'm not sure that is the correct answer for me. I don't want a bunch of women trying to fix or pity me. I will pray about it, and then I'll let you know."

Gail smiled. "You are a wise woman. Praying about it is the best way to approach this."

Reverend Peters's voice wafted into the hallway, saying a prayer to close the evening. I had to admit that I had enjoyed myself. But what was going to stick with me was Gail's idea that I needed to talk about my trauma with other people. She was, in essence, encouraging me to face my biggest fear of others knowing about my past.

Chapter 24

I HAD NOT WRITTEN IN MY JOURNAL for a few days, so I made time to do that. I had numerous thoughts on my mind.

Am I enough? This question continues to haunt me. Anna, Sarah, Ellie, and even Jordyn at her young age also seem to be plagued by this question. Their feelings align with my own. Am I enough without my powerful career? Am I enough with my little business and my little income? With all the trauma I've experienced in my life, can I ever be whole and complete? Doubt and questions continue to fill my waking thoughts and dreams.

But then, I recently read a book by Henri Nouwen. Something he said struck me. He said we believe the lies that others tell us, while we doubt the truths that God knows and tells us. We believe other people and we doubt God! Those lies from other people and society feed my own critical voices. For some reason, the lies seem to be easier to believe and harder to forget than the loving messages that God shares. Both Mrs. Dalton and Mr. Carroll told me I am enough because I'm made in God's image. Is that part of God's truth? I wonder. It doesn't seem possible that as flawed as I am, I could possibly be made in the image of God.

Of course, believing Satan's lies is not a new problem. It is a problem as old as humanity. Satan wants me to believe that I'm not enough so that I will be distracted from God and will instead put all my energy on trying to achieve the next item or goal on my list. Satan doesn't want me to understand the truth that I'm enough because I'm a child of God and not because of my accomplishments, so he will keep distracting me with lies.

We humans have a deep desire to be worthy and to be enough, but for most of us, it doesn't seem possible. And lately, my feelings of being unlovable and unworthy make it easier to believe these lies than to believe God's truth.

I took a deep breath and paused for a moment before finishing this entry.

As I sit here writing, I wonder how I move away from believing what others and my inner voices tell me to believing what God tells me instead. Perhaps this will be the biggest lesson to be learned.

I closed my journal. These thoughts of doubt, and of being enough and being made in God's image were deep. I needed to continue discussing these ideas with someone else. I just couldn't wrap my mind around it all. My brain hurt and my body ached as well, so I decided to lie down and relax. I closed my eyes and took slow, deep breaths.

As I relaxed in my bed, I replayed what Gail had said about

needing to share my trauma with other people. Was she right? Is it difficult to heal from trauma when it is a secret? It made sense that to heal, I needed to get it out in the open instead of allowing it to hold me hostage to fear. But the thought of telling other people about being raped terrified me. What if they didn't believe me? What if this confirmed to others that I was unlovable? I was shocked that I had told Gail in the first place, but the idea of telling even more people sent shivers down my spine. And who would I tell? I had no idea. I just knew I didn't want to talk about it in a group. I would rather think about sharing with a couple of trusted people.

Lying down had obviously not stopped my overactive brain. I turned on some classical music to help me relax. I focused on my breathing and on the music. Each time a thought came to my mind, I told myself it could wait until tomorrow. Before I knew it, an hour had passed, and I had relaxed into a nice nap.

Chapter 25

I HAD YET AGAIN IGNORED the weeds in the flower beds for too long. As I glanced at them, I wondered how I would ever win this battle. Perhaps the job could not be completed in one day, but I knew I could at least make an improvement.

As I worked, I thought about Ellie and Jordyn. They both faced difficult challenges. I wondered how I could help them realize how much they were loved and appreciated not just by their family and friends, but by God. My heart especially went out to Jordyn. The teenage years were always challenging, and she had the extra burden of processing her parents' divorce.

Emotions swirled inside of me as I continued to pull out weeds. I thought back to the pain I had carried throughout my own teen years and beyond. I wondered again what someone could have said back then to help me. When I was a teenager, I did not believe anyone who tried to tell me that God loved me. The walls I had built around my soul were formidable. But my loving family had planted a seed of love and faith in my heart. Observing my grandmother's faith was a wonderful example for me even at a time when I had closed off my soul to God. I prayed that I could somehow plant a seed for Jordyn too.

My thoughts then shifted from past pains to more recent ones. I realized that the phone call from my former partner had triggered the doubts, fears, and priorities I'd held in my past, including in my past career. I had thought this earlier, but now I knew with conviction that I was correct. And then the confrontation with Clark in the parking lot triggered my past trauma responses and all the negative emotions tied to them. Even my conversations with Ellie and Jordyn occasionally brought up painful feelings for me. Perhaps what I was feeling was PTSD or something similar. That would explain why these old feelings were back. In a way, I was facing the pain, fears, and traumas again. It didn't mean that the healing I had worked on over the last year was back to square one. It simply meant that I had again faced triggers that reminded me of my past. It felt better to realize my progress over the last year was not wasted, but I knew I needed to keep working through these current events and renewed feelings. After all, I didn't want to live behind a wall again. I needed to face these issues and learn strategies to help me address these emotions going forward.

In the flower bed, I looked down and saw a huge weed in front of me. I wrapped both hands around it and pulled with all my strength, but it wouldn't budge. Determination flooded my body, and I bent down a little further to change my angle and gave it another yank. It took a few minutes, but with work, the weed finally gave up the fight and came flying out of the ground. I fell backward with surprise and suddenly found myself sitting on the ground, still grasping the giant weed. In my shock, I vacillated between wanting to cry from the jarring fall and laughing at the absurdity of it all. After I sat for a minute, I finally threw the weed onto the growing pile, stood up to assess my progress, and smiled. It was amazing how many weeds you could pull when you were processing important issues.

Sam pulled in the driveway as I headed back to the house to clean up. I wiped the dirt from my hands onto my shorts and walked over to his truck.

"Hi, Sam! What are you up to today?"

"Can't a friend just stop by to say hello?" He grinned at me.

I tried to quickly hide my surprise at his greeting. "Well, of course they can. How are things going?"

Sam looked away from me. It was obvious he noticed my surprised expression. "Everything is great. I thought I'd come take a look at the sweet corn we planted. I wanted to make sure it still looks okay after that heavy rain we had the other day." He paused for just a second and then added, "Want to join me?"

"Absolutely, let's go. Aunt Lu came out the other day, but I confess I haven't checked on it at all."

"Too busy pulling weeds out of the flowers?"

"It's a never-ending job."

"Yeah, it is. I was thinking that Jordyn might be able to help you and Lu when the corn is ready."

"That would be great. Shucking all that corn is hard work. Extra hands would be a blessing."

Sam looked out over the fields. I could tell he had something on his mind, so I just stood and waited. I thought he had caught me off guard with the "friend" comment, but I wasn't at all prepared for what he said next.

"Lydia, I've wanted to ask you something for a long time. I just haven't been able to do it. I, um . . . I'm having a hard time finding the right words, so, well, I'm just going to ask." He paused. Then he took a deep breath and said, "Would you like to grab some dinner sometime? Maybe go to a movie or something together?"

I couldn't speak. I just stood there. I had convinced myself I wasn't ready for a relationship, but I didn't want to hurt his feelings because I cared about him. And I wanted to say yes, but I wasn't ready. Fear coursed through me. What if I ruined everything again? Apparently, this back-and-forth conversation in my head took longer than I realized because the next thing I knew, Sam had started talking again.

"I'm sorry. I never should have asked you out. I know we have a boss-and-employee relationship. I'm sorry if I crossed a line. I promise it won't happen again." He turned and walked toward his truck.

He had already taken several steps before I found my voice. "Sam? Sam, stop. Please don't go. Let me explain," I said, hurrying to catch up with him.

"No need to explain. You either agree that I crossed a line, or you simply aren't interested in me. It's okay. I need to go anyway."

"Sam, please stop. It's very complicated. Please let me say something." My mind raced. What should I say? Should I just explain everything? That might scare him off permanently. How would he react to my past? Questions flew through my head so fast that I had a hard time even recognizing all of them. I finally quieted my thoughts long enough to be able to speak again.

"Thank you for stopping," I said, swallowing down as many emotions as I could. "It's just that . . . I have demons in my past. One of the reasons I moved back here was because this slower and quieter pace of life is letting me face those demons. Even now, I've recently realized they are still haunting me, and I still have work to do. It wouldn't be fair to either of us if I agreed to go out right now." I looked at the ground. "You see, I'm a broken woman."

When I looked up at Sam, I thought I saw conflict in his eyes. I wondered if he was debating whether or not to believe me. I definitely saw pain in his eyes. I realized I had hurt him, and that was horrible to acknowledge.

Finally, he said, "Lydia, we're all broken. We need to help and support each other as we heal. Look, I have to go."

I didn't move as he climbed into his truck and drove off without saying another word. I desperately wanted to chase him and say, *Yes. Yes, I want to go out with you.* But I was frozen to the ground. An inner voice said it was for the best. There was no need to bring him into the chaos of my life. I began to cry, and I wandered aimlessly around the farm. A part of me hoped I hadn't lost my only chance with Sam.

Then I remembered again what Clark had yelled. I told myself that Sam probably wouldn't want to go out with me if he heard what Clark said. I was sure the entire town would find out soon, and I would be the laughingstock of the community. Or at least I would be the new hot gossip story. Sam probably wouldn't want to be associated with me then. Clark was right. I was nothing in high school, and nothing had changed.

I thought of nothing else the rest of the day. My thoughts followed me to bed, and I did something I had not done in a long time. I cried myself to sleep.

After yet another restless night, I knew I needed to talk to someone. Thankfully, it was the weekend, so I hoped Gail might have some free time. I was struggling to forget the look of pain in Sam's eyes. I had hurt him by rejecting his date idea, and that hurt me deeply. She could hear how upset I was when I called her and told me to come right over.

As soon as I saw Gail, I began to cry. I told her that Sam had asked me out, and that it had taken me forever to respond because I was trying to decide what to share with him. Then, I told her that I'd said I couldn't go out with him right now because I was a broken woman. I sobbed when I recounted that he'd said we are all broken and that we need to help and support each other as we heal.

"Then he left, and I just stood there. Gail, I let him go without saying anything else. The pain in his eyes was . . . well . . ." I struggled to speak but finally said, "I hurt him deeply."

"Did you tell him that you are working on healing?" she asked.

"Yes. And that's when he said we are all broken."

She nodded. "That is true. We each have our own brokenness." She didn't speak for a few minutes, seemingly lost deep in thought.

"You know, we discussed that many years had passed between the time when you experienced your traumas and when you began to face them. That means you've been told lies by yourself, by others, and by Satan for just as long. One of Satan's favorites is that there's something about us that keeps us from experiencing love. It's going to take time to replace all of those lies in your mind with God's truth. I know it's easy for me to tell you that you are enough and that you are loved. I also recognize it's much more difficult for you to believe that and to know it in your soul."

"Maybe I need a sign I can look at every day," I suggested.

Gail smiled. "That's a great idea! Put it in a prominent place so that you can gaze on it frequently." She paused for a minute and then said, "You also need to remember something else we've discussed. Another lie that you've believed."

"What's that?"

"That any new relationship you begin will end as your past relationships have. That's a fearful voice from the past that is trying to protect you from the pain you've experienced over and over. You are not the same woman, but that old voice doesn't realize that."

I couldn't speak as realization washed over me. Gail was correct. I wasn't the same woman. I shouldn't continue living in fear and listening to voices that only knew my past.

Then Gail added, "I also want to go back to what I told you earlier. I honestly believe you need to share your trauma with other people. I don't know how many, and I don't know who. But it feels like keeping it a secret is keeping you in bondage to it. You are afraid that others will find out, and so you haven't fully released it. And now with Clark's threat, it's a fresh wound. This may be another part of why you're afraid of having a relationship with Sam. You may be worried that if your secret is exposed, then Sam might abandon you too."

"Yes. I've been thinking about all you have said, but I still don't think our small group is the correct group to share this with."

"It doesn't have to be that group. And maybe you only need to share it with one or two people."

I nodded. "I'll pray about how to move forward and about who I trust enough to share this with. But one last thing."

"What's that?"

"How do I respond to Sam? I can't leave him like he is right now."

Gail didn't answer me with words. Instead, she gave me a hug. Driving home, I asked God to help guide me and to help me handle my fears. I also prayed that answers would come soon because it broke my heart to think of how I'd left things with Sam.

Chapter 26

ELLIE HAD NOT ATTENDED our most recent small group gathering, and I hadn't talked to her for a few days. I wanted to know how she was doing, but I had been avoiding her because I was avoiding Sam. I called her when I finally realized I was being ridiculous and immature, but it immediately went to voicemail. She didn't get back to me for a couple of days, and when she did, she apologized for the delay.

"It's okay. I know you're very busy these days," I reassured her.

She sighed and said, "I'm exhausted. I'm working overtime, and I'm afraid that means I'm ignoring things at home that I should be doing."

"Is there anything I can do to help?"

She was quiet for a while and then asked, "Would you be willing to take Jordyn shopping for some new clothes?"

"You need to know that my experience shopping for myself is minimal. I'm not sure how helpful I would be, but I'm happy to take her."

"Jordyn has definite opinions on her clothes. Honestly, she only needs transportation, some conversation, and the occasional veto for something too pricey. I will give her cash, and I will tell her that when it's gone, the shopping trip is over."

"I enjoy spending time with her, so I would love to take her if you think she'd be okay with it."

"She likes spending time with you too, so I know she will enjoy your time together."

I was relieved when Ellie said she would drop Jordyn off at my house on her way to work. I wasn't ready to face Sam yet, and I was glad I didn't have to pick her up at his house.

Jordyn was quiet on our drive to the mall. We'd driven for at least fifteen minutes when I pointed it out to her.

"Oh. I guess I don't have anything to say," she said.

"Is everything okay?" I asked.

"Yeah."

"So, we're back to one-word answers?" I joked.

She gave me a small smile. "I just can't think of anything to say."

"Ah. As a lawyer, I was trained to always have something to say," I explained.

A second smile! Then she said, "Honestly, everything is fine. It all seems the same as it's been since we moved in with Uncle Sam. Did you know he hates it when I call him that? He asked me to just call him Sam, but mom thinks that's disrespectful. But it seems to me that it's more disrespectful to call him something he doesn't like."

"That's wisdom, Jordyn. How's it going with all the hours your mom is working? She told me she's working overtime."

"Yeah. I'm alone all the time, but that's not much different than before. Mom and Dad always seemed to be focused on their own stuff and ignored me. They never seemed interested in spending time with me."

Though Jordyn didn't use the word *abandonment*, it sounded

like that was exactly what she meant. Abandonment was something I had felt repeatedly in my life. I had felt abandoned by the deaths of loved ones and by every boyfriend I'd ever had. And for years after the rape, I had felt abandoned by God. During my lowest moments, I was certain He had abandoned me as so many others had already done. It was only in the last year that I realized He had not abandoned me at all, and scripture promised me He never would. But since so many others had, I was still afraid something might cause it to happen. It was one of my own greatest fears.

A few miles went by while I debated what to say next. I decided to be honest, but I began small. If she seemed uncomfortable, I would stop.

"Jordyn, I know it seems as if your parents didn't want to spend time with you, but I don't think that's the entire truth. I believe they both love you very much, but their struggles have preoccupied them. I think they've been going through some difficult times, and they don't know how to process all of it. And I'm sure they want to protect you from feeling their pain. Even if that didn't work, it might be what's happened."

"Why couldn't they just tell me that?" she asked.

"People like to hide their problems, especially from their children. I'm guessing they didn't want to place their burdens on you. And maybe they didn't even have the words to say it."

"Do other people do that? Or just my parents?"

"I would say most people are like your parents," I said.

"Does that mean there are a lot of kids like me who feel ignored?"

"It's not just kids who feel ignored and abandoned. Many adults do too. More than you could ever imagine."

She took a deep breath, paused a moment, and then asked,

"Do you think my parents feel abandoned?" It was an insightful question.

"It's very possible that they do."

Several more miles passed as she considered this revelation. And then she proved what an amazing person she was. "When I see my mom tonight, I'm going to give her a hug and tell her I love her."

I glanced over at her and smiled. "She would love that."

"Have you ever felt ignored and abandoned?" she asked.

"Yes, I have. Even as an adult. Feeling abandoned hurts. The pain can cut right through you. There was even a time when I thought God had abandoned me, but He hadn't. I was so focused on my problems and my pain that I didn't realize God was right there with me."

From the corner of my eye, I saw Jordyn studying my face. She looked like she had heard what I'd said and was thinking about it.

When we arrived at the mall, I asked Jordyn where we should begin our shopping. She suggested we park by the food court so that we could treat ourselves when we were done. I told her I liked her way of thinking.

We deserved the ice cream cones we bought after all the shopping we did. Ellie was correct that Jordyn had ideas about her clothes. She tried on so many outfits that I was exhausted for her. In the end, she bought two pairs of shorts and three tops. Not only did she know what she liked and what she needed but she was also a smart shopper looking for sales. We decided to sit on a bench and enjoy our cones.

"I'm glad we decided to sit down and enjoy our ice cream. Otherwise, it would probably be dripping all over me while I drove. I'm not always a neat eater."

"I couldn't wait to try this. I've never tried chocolate overload!" she said, attacking her ice cream with fervor.

"And? Do you like it?"

"It's amazing. Thank you for buying it. And thanks for taking me shopping. Mom said some of my clothes were just too worn out to wear."

"I had a great time today. I enjoyed shopping, and I always enjoy our talks."

"Me too, Lydia." She stopped eating her ice cream and looked at me. "It's nice to have a grown-up to talk to. I mean, a grown-up who listens and thinks I have something to say. Thank you."

"I'm always available. Anytime you want to talk, just call me." At that moment, a big blob of ice cream fell on my pants. "Ugh! Well, since I'm in public, I will let that blob go." I used a napkin to clean up the mess.

She laughed and added, "If your ice cream is as good as mine, that takes some strong willpower."

We finished our desserts and walked back to the car. Conversation flowed much more easily on the drive home, and we talked about school and the music Jordyn liked. Ellie had arrived right before we did, and Jordyn jumped out of the car to show her mom her purchases. I rolled down my window and said, "We had a great time, and it's all my fault if she doesn't want dinner."

I was still stuffed from my ice cream cone, but I sat with Aunt Lu while she ate her dinner. She wanted to hear all about the shopping trip, and I was glad to tell her what a wonderful time we'd had. We cleaned up the kitchen for the day, and I had just sat down to enjoy a nice glass of wine when the doorbell rang. It was Ellie.

"I desperately need to talk to someone. Are you busy?"

"Not at all. Would you like a glass of wine? I just poured myself one."

She stood staring at me without a word. I was confused as to why this was a difficult question. She finally answered, "Do you have any coffee?"

"Of course. Let me make a pot. Regular or Decaf?"

I made idle conversation while I got the coffee and the filters out of the cupboard and poured the water into the coffee maker. Since it would take a few minutes to brew, I asked if she wanted to sit at the kitchen table.

"Sure. That works," she replied.

"I'm just going to come right out and say that you don't sound like yourself. Is everything okay?"

She sighed. "Sam and I just had an argument. He confronted me about a few things, and I needed to get out of there."

"Do you want to talk about the argument?"

She dropped her head into her hands and said, "I'm not sure where to begin. He doesn't think I'm handling things very well. And he says I'm drinking too much. He even said he thinks I may be an alcoholic."

Ah, I thought to myself. *That explains why my question about wine was greeted with confusion.* "How do you feel about how you're handling things?"

"How are you supposed to handle divorce? How are you supposed to handle it when your husband doesn't think you're enough anymore and cheats on you with multiple women?"

"I don't have all the answers, Ellie. Obviously, I haven't

been through a divorce. But I have experienced pain and broken relationships. The one thing I know is that we can't hide or run from the pain. We need to sit down with it, face it, and process it. We can't turn to something that allows us to avoid it. I've spent most of my life running and hiding from pain and fear, and I can tell you it only makes things worse. I also know this—God will sit with us in our pain. He didn't cause it, but He will sit with us as we're going through it. And I will sit with you too."

She began to cry. We sat in the kitchen with her coffee getting cold and my wine getting warm, and she cried for a long time. I wasn't sure I had enough tissues for all these tears. Eventually, she looked up at me with the saddest expression I'd ever seen. Her broken heart was visible in her eyes.

I moved my chair closer and hugged her. I hadn't thought she could sob any harder at that point, but I was wrong. Ellie had cried before, but there was something deeper in it this time. It dawned on me that we were on holy ground. She trusted me with her raw emotions. I was a safe landing place for her to face her pain and share it. It was an honor to have someone trust me in that sacred moment.

Eventually her tears slowed and finally they stopped. We simply sat and said nothing. Facing deep pain was exhausting. Even though I prayed for the right words to say, nothing came to me. I decided it was better to sit in silence. Eventually, she whispered hoarsely, "Thank you."

"I'm glad to sit with you in this difficult time."

"Thank you for sharing your experience with running and hiding. That gives me the courage to face this."

"I'm sure you know this, but it's not a one-and-done deal.

I'm constantly facing my pain. It gets better, but it takes work and time."

"I know. And I also know that I have been using alcohol to hide from my pain. The wine not only numbs it, but occasionally, I can even forget about it," she admitted.

"So true. Our addictions only numb and distract us. If we keep turning to them, then the pain and trauma are still in control. That's not healthy, and it keeps us from really living. We are only surviving, and that's no way to live."

Ellie blinked back a new wave of tears. "I know I still have healing to do," she said. Then she added, "I also want to tell you that I'm so glad we've become friends."

"Me too," I replied.

We sat in the kitchen until she realized that she needed to get home to check on Jordyn. I said goodbye, and then I sat at the kitchen table again and prayed for Ellie to have the courage to face all her pain. She had a long and difficult journey ahead of her, but I knew she was up to it.

Then I remembered my conversation with Gail about our internal voices. Those voices were part of my trauma, so I needed to address them. These voices knew I had faced considerable pain in my past relationships, and they were trying to protect me. Though they may have been trying to protect me from making the same mistakes, they weren't helping me now because they didn't have the full story. They only knew the past. They knew nothing of the future, and they certainly didn't understand the growth I had experienced.

As far as the external critics like Clark were concerned, they were just trying to cause me pain. Clark didn't have the full story either. And maybe he was in pain and wanted everyone else to be in pain with him. I would need to pray about how to respond to him too. I knew I would have more interactions with him in the future, and I needed to be prepared to respond in a way that honored the woman I was now.

I also had to talk to Sam somehow. What could I say? Would he even be willing to listen to me? I knew I couldn't continue to ignore him or allow us both to suffer with this unresolved issue between us.

Chapter 27

GAIL AND I TYPICALLY MET about thirty minutes before our small group meeting to review our plans for the upcoming session. We also prayed for each of the women who had been attending. Gail mentioned that she would like to take the lead at this meeting. She had recently read a wonderful book and wanted to share and discuss a quote from it. I was getting ready to ask her about it when Ellie entered the room.

"I hope it's okay that I came early," she said. "I didn't have enough time to go home and come back, so I thought I would come now."

Gail smiled and replied, "Of course it's okay. We're so glad you're here. Would you both excuse me for a minute? I forgot to refill my water bottle. I'll be right back."

Ellie sat down and sighed. "Lydia, I know this isn't the appropriate place or time to discuss this, but I've been working such long hours, and I haven't had time to call since we last talked at your house. Clark is acting horribly again. He's threatening to sue for full custody of Jordyn. Apparently, he's also told his lawyer that you are a horrible person and that our divorce is your fault. I don't know what to do. I'm angry and distraught that he is using our daughter as a pawn in a proceeding that is about the two of us."

"Ellie, I am so sorry. I should have told you before, but he verbally attacked me in public. I thought he would come after me individually, not make me part of your case. Let's find time in the next couple of days to talk. I will also make some calls to see if there is anything we can do to stop this from spirally further downward."

"Thank you. I don't think I could face this without you by my side. I'm sorry he's dragged you into this. Usually, he saves his nastiness for me. I think he's a little intimidated by you, so maybe he thinks if he can hurt you, you might drop my case."

"We'll face this challenge together. After I make those calls, I'll let you know what I've learned," I said.

Ellie pulled a tissue from her purse and dabbed at her eyes. I was absorbed in my own thoughts for a minute or two. I wondered who Clark had already told about my past and how long it would take for the entire town to hear it. After all these years, I wondered if anyone would care. All I knew for sure was that I cared. I felt my shame and anxiety building as I thought about the what-ifs. Once again, I realized that my worst fear was playing out.

When Gail walked back into the room, I put my thoughts aside as Ellie started to tell Gail and me what was new with Jordyn and how she was adjusting. We then talked about random subjects as you do when you're passing time. Finally, the rest of the group began to wander in, and they each shared a little update about their lives since our last meeting. It was comfortable conversation among a group of women who were quickly becoming very good friends. We were all excited to hear that Sarah had an interview scheduled. And Anna shared that she felt she was coping with her approaching empty nest, but she was still struggling. When everyone had arrived, Gail asked the group to pause for a quick prayer. Then she began a meeting that I can confidently say changed my life.

"Friends, we have discussed many things since we began meeting as a group, and I believe we have all seen a common theme. Most—and perhaps all—of us believe in some way that we are not enough on our own. Furthermore, we believe our unworthiness is the source of many of our problems. Please listen now if you haven't truly heard this before. That is a lie. It is Satan's lie. You are enough. If we look to the Bible, there are numerous passages that tell us this, if not the entire Bible.

"I want to remind you of the very first chapter in the Bible. Lydia and I have talked about this, and I want to share it with all of you as well. The first chapter of Genesis tells us that we are made in God's image. I believe that this is crucial. Being made in God's image most definitely means that we are enough. Now, I want to share a quote with you. I pray that this helps you to further believe that you are enough and that you are worthy.

"This is a quote by Henri Nouwen. I enjoy his writing, and you might want to read some of his wonderful books. Okay, here's the quote: 'If I am the beloved of God, how do I claim my belovedness? I begin by daily repeating the very words Jesus heard at his baptism, for they are also meant for me and for you: You are my beloved. With you I am well pleased.'"

Gail paused to let these words sink in. I wondered what expression my face was showing, because the inside of me was shocked. I had never heard this point of view. Did God intend those words for me as well as for Jesus? Internally, my soul began to weep.

Gail finally spoke again. "Who can possibly believe they aren't enough when God has told each of us that He is pleased with us?

God saw all that He had made, and it was good. God created you and has proclaimed—with you I am well pleased. How can we possibly believe Satan's lies that we aren't enough and that God is withholding something from us when God made us in His image and said He is pleased with us? Perhaps this evening you cannot fathom what this means for yourself. I encourage you to pray about this quote and reflect on how it might speak to you. I want it to fill your soul. I know it might be easier to say these words than to believe and feel them, and that's why I want you to pray about it. I pray that you can understand this not just in your head, but that you sincerely feel it in your soul."

Conversations swirled around me. I could hear their voices, but I could not understand what they were saying. The only thing I heard over and over was, *You are my beloved. With you I am well pleased.* A voice deep inside me kept repeating it, and then would add, *Yes, my dear Lydia, with you I am well pleased.*

The other women were standing up and leaving, and still I sat. Finally, Gail and I were the only ones left in the room. She came to sit beside me for a while before she spoke.

"Are you okay, my friend? You haven't said anything, and you haven't moved."

"I don't know what to say," I replied. I sat for a while longer. Then, I looked at her and asked, "Do you believe that quote? Do you believe that God intended that quote for you and me and not only for Jesus?"

"I believe it deep in my soul. When I read that quote for the first time, I wept. God's peace washed over me when I read it, and I felt an amazing blessing. He made me in His image, and I am His beloved. And He is pleased with me." She smiled. "Perhaps

He isn't pleased with everything I do and say, but in me, He is pleased."

"I can't describe what, and I can't describe how, but this has changed me," I said. "I can't even find the words to describe what I'm feeling, but I know it has changed me. I feel like something has shifted inside me. I wish I could find the words to explain it."

"I can tell that it has. As it has changed me," she said.

We then prayed for each other and for each of the women in our group. After our final *amen*, we stood and left the church. In some way that I couldn't describe, I walked out a different woman.

The number of thoughts running through my mind the next morning almost made me dizzy. Journaling was the only solution I could think of to process them. I decided to play some music as I wrote. One of my grandmother's old gospel albums seemed like a good choice. Her record player looked almost as old as a Victrola, and I was thrilled it still worked. The first song on the record was "Precious Lord, Take My Hand."

Grandmother had loved that hymn. I smiled as I remembered her saying in times of stress, "Precious Lord, here's my hand." Grandmother had records by various artists that included this song. It was one of those songs that could be interpreted in many ways. It could be slow and mournful, or it could be upbeat and jazzy. I always enjoyed the upbeat interpretations, and I was pleased that the version on this recording was one of my favorites. I started the record and then went to my desk to write.

So much to process. So much to write. Yes, precious Lord,

please take my hand and lead me. Thoughts and emotions continued to swirl, so I just decided to begin. Perhaps some discernment would come during the writing process.

Enough. That theme continues to be an ocean wave ebbing and flowing around me. This belief that we are not enough goes back even to Adam and Eve, and their story, of course, also centers around the theme of shame. It seems that my struggles run parallel to theirs, and perhaps that is true of everyone.

I've listened to Satan's lies for years—lies about not being worthy and that I'm unlovable and that my past prevents me from being God's beloved. Satan fills us all with lies and distractions. I need to learn to recognize them as lies.

I think part of the reason people think they aren't enough is that they try to compare God's love to human love. Human relationships are often based on conditional love. That is why we work so hard to be loved and accepted. Perhaps this is one reason why self-help books are so popular. We are all trying to be loved and to make someone stay in love with us. We are terrified that we will lose someone's love, but God's love isn't like that. It is unconditional. I can't earn it, and I can't lose it.

I paused to read what I had written. Some interesting thoughts had already occurred to me as I wrote, and I still wanted to ponder on the Henri Nouwen quote Gail had shared. I was going to start my journal writing with that quote, but it honestly frightened me a bit. It was a life-altering moment for me, and I didn't know if I could find the right words to describe how I was feeling. I decided to try anyway.

You are my Beloved. With you I am well pleased.

Tears ran down my face. I put the pen down as I reached for a tissue. I didn't try to fight these tears or even try to understand them. I let them come. It would take time to fully understand what this quote meant to me, but it was transformational. I picked up my pen again and searched for the words I needed.

This quote from Henri Nouwen has transformed me deeply. I don't fully understand what has changed yet, but I want to capture in words what I'm feeling today. As I have written before, I have repeatedly heard that I am made in God's image. And since I'm made in God's image, I'm enough. I'm worthy. It has been difficult for me to move that idea from my head to my soul. Satan's lies, society's expectations, and my own internal critics have made it difficult to believe that I'm enough just the way I am.

Nouwen's quote has made the idea of being made in God's image come alive for me. But perhaps the most meaningful part of this quote is that God is pleased with me. God says I am worthy and enough, not because of anything I have done, but because I'm His beloved. Every time I hear that, I begin to cry. It doesn't matter what society says or what any person says. It doesn't matter about my traumatic past. God is pleased. I have spent most of my life trying to achieve something so that people would accept me and find me to be worthy. But God has proclaimed this to be true simply because I am. Because I am His beloved.

And now I ask myself, how will I live my life differently?

I put my pen away and closed my journal. Suddenly, I knew the first thing that I would do: I had to share my secret. Gail was correct. Keeping the trauma a secret was keeping me in bondage to it. Sharing this secret would require me to face my fear of letting others know about it, but I was convinced it would allow for deeper healing. I had worried about what Clark might say about my past, but even he didn't know the entire story. For me to share this secret would mean I would need to share it all. I had to find the courage to face my fears of someone knowing the whole truth about my past.

I took a deep breath as I realized who I had to share this with: Sam. I had to tell him everything if I wanted to pursue a relationship with him. I was afraid, but I decided I would no longer allow potential pain and fear to rule my life. If Sam rejected me when he learned about my past, I knew I would be okay because God loved me. I had to release this poison so that it would no longer affect me. I would lean into my pain and fear by telling Sam. It was the only way I could possibly move forward.

Chapter 28

SCENARIO AFTER SCENARIO played out in my mind as I wandered around the yard. Should I call Sam and talk to him over the phone? Should I drive to his house? The options were endless, and I weighed the pros and cons of each one. I couldn't decide if I was obsessed about how I should tell him to avoid talking to him or if it was because I wanted to make this conversation as painless as possible for both of us. As often happens, none of the scenarios in my mind came to fruition because he drove in just as I reached the orchard. I walked toward him, and I didn't give him a chance to speak.

I immediately said, "Sam, I'm glad you're here because I need to talk to you. Please don't say anything until I'm done because I need to get all of this out. Why don't we sit under a tree? Or better yet, follow me. Let's climb up this tree. I'll sit on this branch, and you can sit on that one."

He raised his eyebrows at me. "You want me to climb a tree so we can talk?"

"Yes. It's a crazy idea for a serious conversation. I need my wonderful trees for support."

"Good grief. You have me worried," he replied.

We climbed to our assigned branches, and I began to pray

for the right words and for courage. I started to cry before the conversation even began.

"Oh, Lydia. This is why we should be on the ground. I could give you a handkerchief or something."

"There will be many more tears before this conversation is over," I said. I took a deep breath and then dove in.

"Sam, I've wanted to go out with you for months. But as I told you, I have demons from my past that I need to work through. After considerable thought and prayer, I've realized that keeping those things a secret only keeps the pain buried. This allows the trauma to stay in control, and I don't want that any longer. Also, I'm telling you all of this, but I won't be telling everybody." I looked up at Sam on his branch, and he nodded his understanding and agreement.

"These things have haunted me for years. If I have any hope of having a relationship with you or anyone else, I need you to know this. Years ago, I was raped. I'm not sure I can find the words to tell you how shattered I was. I lived a broken existence for more years than I want to admit. That trauma then led me to make many poor choices in the guys that I dated and in my actions with them. I'm ashamed of it, but that was how I reacted to the trauma. I kept looking for someone who would heal my pain. Instead, it just kept growing. I ended up building walls around myself to try to shut it out, but that only kept it in. I was looking for healing from a person, and my shame kept me from turning to the true healer. It wasn't until I moved back here that I realized God loved me. I've been on a journey to wholeness with God ever since. Recently, I've realized I still have pain and fears to work through. Who knows? Maybe it will take the rest of my life. I know I'm in a better place, but I still have work to do."

I stopped talking and let my emotions flow out of me. I had been afraid that I would be sobbing and unable to speak, but instead, these were gentle tears of relief, not tears of pain or fear. I looked up at Sam and saw him wipe at his own eyes. We sat quietly for a few minutes. As I leaned into the tree, I reflected on the peace I was feeling instead of wondering about Sam's inevitable response.

Eventually, in a soft voice full of compassion, Sam said, "Lydia, I already knew. I didn't know you were in that kind of pain, but I knew about the rape. Well, I suspected. That jerk you went out with in high school didn't act like it was rape, but I suspected it was because of how you acted around him. I told him to shut up, but I should have made him stop talking. I knew about the other guys too. I just thought you were going through a rebellious stage. I had no idea you were hurting so badly. Even now, I sort of want to go and beat up some of those guys for taking advantage of you."

I quietly chuckled. "Oh, Sam. Maybe I could have used a knight in shining armor back then, but today, well, I guess I would say God's redemption is the knight in shining armor I've been looking for all my life."

Sam nodded and was quiet for a while. "I don't know if this is what you need to hear, but I already know about the trauma, and I would still like to go out with you. That is, if you would like to go out with me."

"Yes. I would like that very much."

"Can we get out of this tree now?"

"Don't you find that the trees give you strength and are like an anchor for you?" I asked.

"Right now, I'm finding that this tree is causing me some pain in the backside."

I laughed harder than I'd laughed in a long time as I jumped out of the tree. Sam was grinning when he jumped down too.

"Of all the things I thought I would do today, sitting in a tree wasn't anywhere on my list," he said.

"These trees bring me such comfort. I can't think of anywhere else I could've had that conversation."

Sam stood and gazed at me, but he was no longer smiling. "I would love to kiss you right now. In fact, I would love to kiss and hug you until all that pain is gone, but my gut tells me that we need to take this slow. I don't want to rush anything and potentially ruin it."

"Thank you, Sam. You're right. I want to take things slowly. I don't want to mess this up either."

"We will take this as slow as we need."

Sam needed to get back to work, and so did I. So we decided on a day when we could go out for dinner, and then he left. After he was gone, I stood there. Unable to move. I cared about Sam and did not want to cause either of us harm. My history with relationships was horrible, and the fear of pain from a failed relationship raced through my body.

"God, I'm going to need your help with this. I'm in unfamiliar territory. Please guide us." My anxious feelings were calmed, and I knew that God was answering my prayer. "Thank you." I wiped away another tear as I went back to the house.

I wondered if I needed to share my trauma with anyone else. The answer came quickly and clearly: I needed to tell Aunt Lu. I looked up at the house and prayed, "God, please be with us. This will be hard for her to hear."

Aunt Lu was where she spent most of the day—in the kitchen. One of our neighbors had some recent health issues, and Aunt Lu thought she needed some dinners to help alleviate her burdens. It looked like every pot and every pan was in use for this project. I went up and put my hand on her shoulder.

"Aunt Lu, can you take a break for a minute?"

She turned around and saw the serious look on my face. "Oh, honey, what's wrong? You look very serious."

"I do need to tell you something, and it is serious. I ask you not to tell others, but I think you should know."

She grabbed the counter for support.

"Let's sit at the table if you are positive you can take a break," I suggested.

"Of course. I can take a break. You've got me worried to death here."

Once we were sitting, I took a deep breath before I began. "Aunt Lu, I just shared something with Sam, and on my way back to the house, I realized that I needed to tell you as well. When I was in high school, a boy I was dating raped me."

Aunt Lu gasped and brought both hands up to her cheeks. Tears flowed down her face, and she closed her eyes as if she was trying to block out what I had just said. Seeing her react this way to my pain caused my eyes to well up. I got up and grabbed a box of tissues from the counter and then pulled one out for each of us. After a moment's pause, I continued my story.

"I was filled with shame about it all, and this, combined with the trauma, led me to make poor choices. I felt abandoned by God, so I turned my back on Him, my family, and my past. That's why I was so distant for so long. Everything felt worse here because this was where it all happened. What I didn't understand until I came back last year was that ignoring the pain only made it worse. I needed to face it and lean into it to be able to move forward in life. I've recently realized that keeping it all a secret gave the trauma power, and so now I've told you and Sam."

Tears continued to roll down Lu's cheeks. "Oh, honey. We all knew something was wrong, but I never thought this. I'm so sorry for what you went through, and I guess I should say for what you are still going through. I'm guessing a trauma like this never completely goes away, and my heart just breaks for you."

I took her hand in mine. "It may not completely go away, but I'm at a point now where I'm not defined by it. It's taken me a very long time to process, and my faith is so important to me now. I can honestly say that I know the peace and the love that can only come from God. I still have work to do, but I greet each day with joy and not dread."

"I've certainly seen a change in you since you've been home."

"God called me to stay here and face my demons. It's been the best decision I've ever made."

Aunt Lu smiled her big, warm smile that could melt an iceberg. "And you've been a blessing to me while you've been here. I'm so glad you've shared this with me. I'm honored that you trust me with your story. And you should be proud of yourself for the courage it has taken to arrive at this point."

I was overcome with emotions, and I was barely able to say thank you. I blew my nose and added, "And I have other news, too."

"Oh, honey, I'm not sure I can handle anything else."

"This is good news. The reason I shared this with Sam is because he asked me out for dinner. I didn't want to begin a relationship with him with this secret between us. We are going to take this slowly and quietly and see what happens."

Aunt Lu jumped up and pulled me to my feet, wrapping me in the biggest bear hug a human could give. "Oh, you are going to make me cry again! That is the best news I've heard in ages. I'm so happy for you. I think he is a wonderful man, and I will pray that it will be a wonderful and healing relationship because I love you both so much!"

We hugged for a few minutes, and when we broke apart, we both looked around at the kitchen.

"Well, Aunt Lu, we've discussed a serious topic and a happy topic, and now I guess it's time to tackle some work," I said.

"I think you're right. We have our work cut out for us to clean up all these dishes."

Chapter 29

THE NEXT DAY, I FELT A NEW lightness in my soul. I decided it would be wonderful to spend time outside, soak in nature, and think about this new feeling. As I walked, I listened to the birds singing and to the wind blowing through the trees. I listened to the music of farm equipment in a distant field. I also listened to my own breathing.

Peace. That was what I was hearing and feeling. I was certain that at least a part of my peace came from telling Sam and Aunt Lu about my demons. Opening up to them meant that I no longer carried the burden of trying to keep my past hidden. It was like sharing my shadow self, the part of me that I had wanted to hide because I thought it made me unlovable. It seemed especially important to release this to someone with whom I hoped to have a relationship. These secrets and trauma were no longer in control, and it also felt like I had released more of my shame. The time and energy I had spent and the worries I'd had trying to keep my secrets were also released by sharing my story. I had not realized how attempting to maintain this privacy had separated me, at least emotionally, from others. I felt a new openness to life, and I was able to breathe deeper.

I reflected on my conversation with Sam. He had already known everything. He knew I had been raped before I had even admitted to myself that's what had happened. He had known about my other relationships too, and he still wanted to pursue a relationship with me. He still reached out to me. He accepted me even though I had made poor choices. I was reminded of Jesus and the Samaritan woman at the well. Jesus knew all about the woman's life, and he still reached out to her. He knew about her relationships with men, but he offered the living water to her anyway. I smiled as I realized Sam was following Jesus's example of loving others who felt unlovable and who had led lives filled with pain.

I had shared my story, and I was still accepted. Those fears of rejection could now be put aside. There was still work to do, but the important point was that I continued to make progress. As I stepped further away from the trauma, the pain lessened even if it wasn't completely gone. In its void, joy was growing in my life.

I celebrated the new inner peace I was experiencing. I honestly didn't know a peace like this was possible. It occurred to me that I should let others, especially Ellie, know that this type of peace was available. It was too life altering to keep to myself.

It crossed my mind that I should call Gail and tell her about my conversations with Sam and Aunt Lu. I knew she would want to know I had shared my secret with them. When I thought she would be home from school, I called her.

"Hi, Gail. Are you sitting down?"

"Oh my. Is this sitting-down thing good news or bad news?" she asked, caution evident in her tone.

"Good news, I think. I did something, and I need to tell you about it," I said.

"I'm sitting now. I think I'm ready to hear it."

"I told Sam everything. I told him my secret," I explained.

"You did! I see now why you weren't quite sure if that was good news or not. It's definitely brave . . . Tell me everything. Where were you? What did you say?"

"I told him in the orchard."

"That makes sense. You love it there."

"Yes, I do. I made him climb a tree with me." I laughed at the memory.

"What?" she exclaimed.

"Sure did. I told him I needed to talk to him about something, and I needed the comfort of my favorite tree to do it."

Gail laughed. Loudly. "I would've loved to have seen that. Two adults up in a tree, just talking. I'm sure it was a sight."

"I never thought about that, but I'm guessing it was." I chuckled again at the image of us that flashed through my mind. How silly had we looked? It didn't matter. "Anyway, I told him everything. The rape and about my actions afterward."

Very quietly, Gail asked, "What was his response?"

"He already knew," I said.

"What do you mean he already knew?"

"The loser who raped me told several guys his side of the story, but Sam suspected by the way I reacted that it was actually rape. That, and the fact that the jerk dumped me right after. He knew about the other guys too. He thought I must have been going through a wild teenage stage, but he didn't know about the depths of my pain. He said he wanted to go beat up some of those guys.

My knight in shining armor wants to defend my honor after all these years."

Gail was very quiet.

"Are you still there, Gail?" I asked after a moment.

"Yes, I'm here. Do you understand the significance of this? He knew, and he still asked you out. Does this help put all those old lies out of your mind? The lies that you aren't worthy, that you are broken, and that no one wants to be with you—are those finally gone?"

"I've learned enough recently to know that those old voices probably aren't gone forever. But in the meantime, I'm counting my blessings, and the biggest one is that God has sent amazing people like you, Aunt Lu, and Sam into my life to help me realize that I am loved."

I could hear Gail sniffle through the phone. "Are you okay? I've been the one doing all the crying lately," I said.

"Oh, Lydia, I think this is just a beautiful story. God has touched my heart with it. I'm amazed, and I guess I would say in awe of this. And I'm so very thankful for God's work in this."

"Me too," I agreed.

Then she added, "Something else occurs to me. Satan lies to us in any way he can. He tells us our past makes us undeserving of God's love and inadequate for what God has called us to do, but he also lies to us about our future because he doesn't want us to become the people God created us to be. He tries to preoccupy us with regrets and worries about our future so that we can't enjoy the present. I think that is what Satan has been doing to you."

Realization flooded through me with her words. "You're right, Gail. I've spent years regretting my past and concerned that someone would discover it. And I've constantly worried that someone who knows about it will try to ruin the life I've worked so hard to build. But now I've found someone I care deeply about who already knew about my past and is still willing to accept me as I am. I told Aunt Lu, too, and her response was amazing. We cried together and I could see her pain for me on her face. I guess I would say it was another holy ground moment."

"Amen, my friend. You have had several of those lately."

I sat smiling when we got off the phone. Conversations with Gail always gave me things to think about. This time, I realized how blessed I was.

Chapter 30

SAM AND I DECIDED WE WANTED to explore our newfound relationship away from the prying eyes of our friends and family. Aunt Lu knew about it and was thrilled for us, but we didn't want others to know just yet. We decided to have dinner at a farm-to-table restaurant in a town about an hour away. Sam loved the idea of not only supporting a local restaurant but an owner who was also raising their own food.

It was possible that someone we knew might be there, but it was less likely than at any of our restaurants at home. Plus, the drive also gave us time to talk. We chatted about the weather and about how it was the constant adversary in the farming world, and we reminisced about sports and some musical events from our high school days. Over the course of the evening, I told him about my former career. He listened attentively as I explained the long hours and the stress of my former life. He didn't know how I stood it as long as I did. That's when I confessed another secret.

"It's another part of the trauma I experienced. To survive, many people who have experiences like mine will turn to addictive behaviors to help cope with the pain. The addiction could be anything—drugs, alcohol, or anything else that appears to dull the pain or distract you from what you're facing. My addiction was work. Society doesn't usually view being a workaholic as an addiction, but it can be. Some people may have admired my work ethic, but it was an addiction for me."

Sam reached across the table and touched my hand. "Lydia, I am so sorry you lived with this pain for so long. I wish I'd known. I don't know what I could have done to help other than sit with you, but I would have done that. And I've never thought of an addiction like this. It's a survival technique to get through the pain every day. I can understand how workaholism is an addiction. With all the hours you worked, there was no time to think about what you went through." He paused for a bit with a faraway expression on his face. "Maybe this explains Ellie's drinking."

I nodded. "Yes, I think it might. She might need to find someone to talk to about what she's facing. Some people think you can pray about the problem and read the Bible and then you'll be cured. That's obviously important, but there's more to it. My faith has helped me immensely, but I still must put in the work to face and process the trauma. Faith isn't a magic pill that fixes you. Faith is what gives me strength, courage, and comfort while I do the hard work. God is my constant companion, but He will not do the work for me. Facing trauma is challenging, and I'm afraid there are people out there, even some professionals, who don't want to do the necessary work to get to the crux of the issue."

"I can understand not wanting to face what's so painful," Sam said.

I nodded again. "It's human nature to avoid pain. It's also important to remember that we can't view one addiction as better than a different addiction. I can't sit here and say, 'Well, I just like to work, and at least I don't do drugs.' Thinking my addiction is better than someone else's won't help me move away from it. It's also easy to make changes to the addiction but still turn to it. You feel that you've changed and are doing better, but you're still not facing the real problem."

"That all makes sense to me."

"Turning to the addiction may seem like it's the easier path to take, but it's not the better path."

Sam nodded.

"There's something else I've learned over the last year," I said.

"What's that?"

"God can handle all our big emotions and doubts and questions. I've had them all, and God hasn't shied away from any of it. Personally, I like to write about what I'm processing. It helps me to see all the issues and dive into them to help me work through them. I know you mentioned doubts and anger about God. I hope you know that God is okay with all of that."

"I haven't done any writing like you do, but I've done thinking and praying. I have a better peace about things now. I know God didn't cause any of these problems, and I do feel God's presence with me. I feel stronger in my faith." Then he paused and looked at me. "This has been a deep conversation, Lydia."

"Yes, it has. I'm sorry. It seems like these types of conversations have become a way of life for me. I've probably bored you to death," I said.

"Not at all, though I would like to find something lighter to talk about. But before we change the topic, I need to ask—would you be willing to talk to Ellie about all of this?"

"We've talked about some of these things, but I can share more with her. If what I've learned can help someone, I'm happy to share."

"Thank you. Now, let's talk about something different. How

about something controversial—like what's your favorite sports team?"

And just like that, we transitioned from a deep, theological conversation to significantly lighter topics. We talked about our favorite sports and teams and about our favorite foods. We also talked about what we enjoyed doing when we had free time. Before we knew it, our server came to let us know the restaurant would be closing soon. We were both shocked when we realized we'd been talking for three hours. Perhaps I shouldn't have been surprised, but I was amazed to discover that we shared many similar tastes and values.

When we got up to leave, Sam took my hand. It seemed like the most natural thing I had ever done.

Chapter 31

I KNEW I NEEDED TO TALK to Ellie again, but I had no idea exactly what I would say. I did know, however, where the conversation should take place: Gentry Woods. It was where I had found my own abundant peace. I called Ellie and told her I would enjoy her company on my next hike. I promised it would be one of the easier trails, and I told her I was positive we would see some beautiful wildflowers. We might even catch an early blooming coneflower variety. I breathed a sigh of relief when she agreed to come along without any argument.

I picked her up, and on the way, we chatted about her job and about Jordyn. Our conversation was relaxed and enjoyable, and I prayed throughout the entire drive that any discussion about serious topics would also be positive. Otherwise, it would be an awkward drive home.

Once we began our hike, I explained to Ellie why I loved it here. "When I'm out in nature, I feel so connected to God. Of course, you can feel that anywhere, but I feel a stronger connection when I'm in nature. I'm surrounded by all this beauty God created. It's almost as if the trees and plants and even the bugs whisper God's truths to me. Plus, I don't have as many distractions when I'm out here. I've found my time here to be so beneficial and important that I schedule time in my calendar for it."

"Maybe I should schedule time like this too. I could use time without distractions. I can't seem to catch my breath anywhere, and it seems like the weight of the world is always on my shoulders. I can already feel myself breathing a little deeper out here," she said.

We walked for a while and then came to one of my favorite spots.

"Let's stop for a bit to fully experience nature," I suggested. "I don't know who thought to put a bench here, but they were brilliant. I've loved this spot in every season on the calendar."

We sat down, and I was intentionally quiet. I wanted Ellie to breathe deeply for a few minutes before I broached our next topic.

I eventually turned to look directly at her. "Ellie, we've talked before about how we can't hide from our pain and about how we need to face it and process it instead. And we've talked about how we've each turned to an addiction to numb the pain and avoid facing our trauma. But trust me on this, the sooner you can lean into the pain and process through it, the better you will be in the long run. I spent years avoiding my pain, and so I basically spent years not truly living."

She shifted uncomfortably on the bench, refusing to meet my eye. She appeared heavily interested in a spot on her shoes.

I kept going. "I've recently learned that there was something else I had to do to keep healing from the trauma. I had to share my secrets with someone else. When I did that, the secrets were no longer in control, and I didn't need to worry about them getting out. I know you've shared some personal things with me, but since I'm your attorney, you know I will hold them in confidence. I wonder if you're still worried about what would happen if others discovered these too. I'm not suggesting you need to tell the world everything, but I encourage you to think about whether sharing your secrets with someone you trust would benefit you as it has me. Obviously, people know about your divorce. I'm referring to the reason and pain behind the divorce. And the drinking too."

Her lower lip trembled. "I'm so ashamed, Lydia. I'm ashamed of my broken marriage and that I turned to drinking to numb myself. It's made me unavailable to my daughter. I pretended I was doing better and had cut back on drinking, but that's not the full truth. Maybe I'm drinking less, but I'm still drinking to avoid facing my problems. I don't know what to do. I know God doesn't give us more than we can handle, but I'm not sure how much more I can take."

I put my arm around her. "I understand. I also used to believe that God gave us only what we can handle, but I don't believe that now because to me, it implies that God caused all the bad things to happen. And I do not and will not believe that. Life is often painful, and I believe with every ounce of my being that God is with us on every step of that painful journey."

"I don't even know where to begin," Ellie said.

"I think you need to find a therapist. Don't give me that *no way* look. If you were having pain in your body, you would go to a doctor. This is no different. There are occasions when we need a professional to help us work through the mess in our lives. A wise person recently shared with me that it's not a character flaw to admit that we need help. It takes courage! You are a courageous woman, Ellie.

"My faith has also been important to me on my journey. I'm not saying that if you pray, God will just take away the pain and that's all there is to it. I don't think that's how this works. What I'm saying is that God will be with you and never leave you."

Ellie sighed. "I don't know. I may be hit by lightning or something, but I'm still mad at God right now."

"I've been there myself. It feels like a frightening place to live, but we aren't the only ones who feel that way. God is okay with our anger. He's big enough to handle all our emotions. What I'm trying to say is that it's okay to be angry at God. He will still be with you."

"How can I know that for certain?" she asked.

"Ask Him," I told her.

"What? I just told you I'm angry at God, and now you're saying I should pray?"

"That's exactly what I'm saying. You could even start by saying, 'God, I'm extremely mad at you right now.' Trust me, I've said it." Ellie looked cynical, and she raised an eyebrow at me.

I silently prayed that I was at least planting a seed. "If you don't feel comfortable praying, you could try writing about it," I suggested. "I've been keeping a journal, and it's helped me. There are times when I just scream at God in my writing."

Ellie sighed and stared off in the distance. When she finally looked at me again, she said, "I guess I've got nothing to lose. I mean, you haven't been struck down yet."

"Nope. I haven't been struck down. I think you will find a sense of peace when you start talking to God in whatever way works for you. There's no right or wrong way. And though I'm no expert, I'm happy to travel along this journey with you and God. I've had friends walk with me on my own path to healing, and I would be honored to walk with you in the same way."

We continued to sit in the sun and soak in our surroundings. I don't know what went through Ellie's mind, but I spent the time just being present and thanking God for this beautiful scenery around me and for this wonderful woman who was quickly becoming a good friend. I prayed for her to be brave and strong enough to be able to face everything she had been through and would still go through.

Finally, Ellie finally spoke again. "Thank you for everything, Lydia. Thank you for sharing that you've also been through trauma and addictions. And thanks for encouraging me to find a therapist. I think I will do that. Even if it's just one time, I will try it. And thank you for being with me through the divorce."

I gently touched her shoulder. "We'll face it all together." I sat for another minute and then said, "Should we get you back home? I don't know how long we've been here, but I don't want anyone worrying about you."

Ellie smiled. "Yeah, Sam might end up calling the police to start a search party."

I needed time alone after my hike, so I sat with my desk chair pulled up to the window in my bedroom. Over the years, I had spent countless hours sitting in this same chair, gazing out this same window. Most of those hours had been spent sitting in the pain of trauma and shame—not processing it, but simply sitting in it, trying to decide what I could have done differently. I wasted so much time listing all the different ways I thought my trauma was my fault and trying to think about all the bad things that could happen to me in the future.

On this day as I sat and reflected, some new thoughts occurred to me. One of the most painful aspects of rape was the loss of control. I had no control and no choice about how someone treated me. I felt humiliated, and the rape caused me years of self-loathing because I always thought I could have or should have done something to stop it. Another painful part was the loss of personhood. When I was raped, I was not truly viewed as a person but instead as an object. It was difficult to find the words to describe that pain. It was worse than not being respected; I was being viewed and treated as less than human, no more important than the carpet I walked across. It hurt, and I mourned for everyone who had ever experienced that pain.

I also thought about the healing I had experienced over the last year. It had allowed me to become open with others, and in turn, others were then able to be open with me. I had never experienced such deep levels of friendship before. In my old life, I had kept everyone at a distance and wouldn't allow anyone to get too close because I didn't feel safe. Once I started my path toward healing, I felt my soul communing with others, and I was able to be present with them. I knew that if I hadn't worked to face my trauma, my relationships would have continued to be shallow. Building this new depth of relationships with others was another blessing in my life.

I had experienced many blessings recently, and I wondered if there was anything I could do to bless others. I smiled as I realized that there *was* something I could do. I would finish my training at the women's center and spend time volunteering there with the survivors.

Chapter 32

SAM AND I DISCUSSED where to go for our next date. We talked about going to a movie, but since we had both been working long hours, we decided that dinner out was all we had the energy for. Neither of us felt like a long drive, so we opted for a closer restaurant this time. I hadn't eaten at this diner in a long time because I wasn't usually in the mood for a "greasy spoon" place, but I had to admit, they served amazing hamburgers.

Our conversation was comfortable as we each shared what we had been working on and how the crops were coming along. We looked over the dessert menu as we finished our dinner, but then I whispered that Aunt Lu had made an amazing pecan bar dessert. That was all Sam needed to hear, and we asked for the check and headed to my house. We took our plates to the porch. It was a beautiful evening, and Aunt Lu's baking did not disappoint.

"I'm sure glad we didn't order dessert at the restaurant. This is incredible," Sam commented between bites. "Your aunt is an amazing cook. She should open her own restaurant."

"I've told her the same thing, but she said that would make it a job and take the joy out of it. In any case, I'm thrilled that we get to enjoy her passion."

We didn't speak as we enjoyed every bite. When we finished eating, we sat for a while. No conversation, just sitting in each other's company. I didn't remember ever sitting with someone, saying nothing, and feeling so content. The evening breeze was refreshing too. I wasn't sure I'd ever had such a quiet and yet completely enjoyable evening. I couldn't hide the smile of joy on my face.

Sam noticed and said, "What are you smiling about? Did I miss something?"

"No. I'm thinking about how I enjoy simply sitting here with you." I felt a sudden wave of anxiety that perhaps I was jumping in too quickly, but Sam's response pushed those thoughts aside.

"I was thinking that too. It's nice sitting here with you. I can just be me and not try to be someone else."

I felt my cheeks flush. "I think that might be the sweetest thing anyone has ever said to me."

"I hope you know you can be authentic around me too," he said.

"I think I'm more authentic with you than I've ever been with anyone, even if I am still a work in progress."

"I understand. And I support you in all you are still processing. And I know we're on a date, but if you don't mind changing the subject a bit for a few minutes, I also wanted to tell you I've noticed a real difference in Ellie recently."

"Oh? What have you seen?" I asked.

"Well, for one thing, she's not drinking anymore. I know she's still hurting, but I see moments of peace and joy too. She seems more relaxed and more like herself again. And the change in her has changed Jordyn too. She's obviously still a moody teenager at times, but she doesn't seem as angry as she was. More like a normal teenager and less like a wounded animal."

Internally, I sighed in relief. It had only been a couple of weeks since our hike, so I was surprised Sam had noticed any changes in his sister yet. I wondered if she had already met with a therapist, or maybe she had considered my suggestion of sharing her secret with others. In any case, I was thrilled that she was experiencing moments of peace and joy and that she wasn't drinking anymore to avoid her problems. It was also wonderful that it was all having a positive impact on Jordyn.

"I'm happy to hear all of that. This is great news."

Sam nodded. "Thank you for spending time with them both and for listening to them."

"I'm honored. Helping them has also blessed me."

Sam nodded again but said nothing else. He didn't need to. We settled into a companionable silence, enjoying the sunset together. Eventually, Sam checked his watch and said he needed to head home.

As he stood to leave, a thought came to me. "There's a music festival over in Pleasant Hill this weekend," I said. "What would you think about going? Maybe we could see if Ellie and Jordyn would like to join us."

"I read about that. Sounds like there will be a wide variety of music. Maybe something for everybody."

"And I bet there will be some yummy food booths too," I added.

He gave me a sheepish grin. "So, I don't know if you've thought about this, but if we take them with us, this will be the reveal of our relationship. And others we know might be there too. Though it's a bit of a drive, this festival always attracts people from around here. Are you okay with people knowing about us?"

I smiled and nodded. "Yes, I'm okay with people knowing."

Sam gave me the biggest smile I had ever seen. Then, to my

pleasant surprise, he leaned over and gave me a quick kiss. "I'm okay with it too. I'll talk to Ellie in the morning to see if she wants to join us. Good night, Lydia."

After Sam left, I sat and reflected on what it would mean for other people to know about our relationship. I was excited but also a bit scared. If other people knew, it would mean our relationship was real. And if it was real, then it was possible that it could end just as all my past relationships had. I took a deep breath and reminded myself that I was not the same person I had been during those old relationships and Sam was not like anyone else I had dated. He was kind, and he was a man of faith. He knew about my past and accepted me as I was. Even still, I had to face these fears.

I was also excited. I cared about him deeply, and I appreciated how different he was from anyone I had previously dated. I loved how Sam's feelings for me mirrored Jesus's love for us. Jesus loves us even at our worst moments. Sam cared for me even knowing about my worst moments. My willingness to enter this relationship was also a reflection of my healing. Previously, I wouldn't have been open to entering a relationship. In fact, I would have run as far as I could in the opposite direction. But now, I looked forward to seeing how we would grow and perhaps even flourish together as I continued to grow and heal.

As for that kiss, our first. There was something so sweet and gentle about the way his lips met mine that it wasn't scary as it might have been in the past. No, this was comforting. Kissing him felt safe, and I smiled as I remembered his promise to take things slowly and at my pace. Still smiling, I went inside and ended a wonderful day.

The weekend arrived and Ellie and Jordyn, Sam, and I all piled into my car. I had offered to drive because I didn't think we would be comfortable crammed into Sam's truck. We packed water bottles and a few snacks in case the food booths didn't look appetizing. As it turned out, we ended up digging into the snacks before we arrived at the festival because Jordyn pointed out that the drive was taking forever and warranted food. She also thought she should provide entertainment for our drive. She shared stories about her music and sports adventures. Most of these stories seemed to involve the long bus trips to these events and the innovative things teens did to pass the time.

When we finally arrived, I had to drive around to find a parking spot, and we were all thrilled when we realized the organizers had arranged for shuttles to take people to the different concert locations. The festival featured several different stages, and each one showcased a different genre, varying from oldies to pop, to country, to rap, and even classical.

"I'm a little overwhelmed with all of the music choices," I shared.

Sam replied, "If you don't mind, I would love to head to the country stage."

"Mom, can we go to the pop concert?" Jordyn begged.

"Sure. We can do that. But would it be okay if we listened to country for just a few minutes? I promise we will move around and listen to your favorites too, but I'm curious what country music they're playing."

"As long as you promise we won't stay there all day, that's okay. I want you to have fun too," Jordyn told her mom.

"It's a deal."

When we reached the country music stage, Jordyn had to tease her uncle. "Are you sure this isn't the 'oldie music'?"

Sam laughed and said, "Are you implying I'm old or something?"

Jordyn didn't say anything, but she couldn't hide her grin.

We had already listened to several songs, when I realized Jordyn and Ellie were still there. It seemed that Jordyn discovered she enjoyed this type of music more than she thought she would.

As I glanced around me, I was overwhelmed by the mass of people. I hadn't been around crowds like that since I'd moved back home, and I quickly realized I enjoyed my new, quiet lifestyle. The crowds and commotion were fine for a day of entertainment, but I admitted to myself that I didn't miss fighting through throngs of people to get to work every day.

"Are you enjoying yourself?" Sam asked. "You've got a big smile."

"I am, but I'm actually thinking about how taxing the noise and energy of this many people are. I don't want to go back to this every day."

He slipped his arm around me. "I'm glad to hear that. I don't want to lose you to the city life."

"No worries about that. I'm definitely enjoying the moment, but I do not miss that old lifestyle."

I looked over at Ellie. Her eyes were glued to the stage and a big smile was plastered on her face. I nudged Sam and nodded toward Ellie. When he saw how happy she looked, he broke into an even bigger smile.

"I'm glad you suggested they come. They both needed something fun to do. I haven't seen her smile like that in a long time," he said.

Finally, we were all tired after a full day of listening to music and being jostled in the crowds. We'd also had our fill of junk food. Between the funnel cake and lemon shake-ups, I'm sure I had consumed a week's worth of sugar in only one day. We squeezed onto a shuttle and made our way back to the car. The drive home seemed to take even longer than the drive to the festival, but we all agreed we didn't want anything else to eat.

I dropped everyone off at Sam's house, and Ellie and Jordyn went inside. Before she reached the door, Jordyn turned around and yelled, "I sure had fun today."

"Me too, Jordyn!" I yelled back.

Sam sat in the car for another minute. "I had fun too. I'm exhausted, but it was a great day." He gave me a quick kiss and then he went inside.

The exhaustion was hitting me fast, but I still smiled as I drove the few miles home. I was glad Ellie and Jordyn had gone with us. Not only did they have a great time, but they also interacted with other people. I thought the day was probably good medicine for them.

One last thought occurred to me as I pulled into my drive. Even though we had seen a few people we knew at the festival, no one seemed surprised to see the four of us together.

Chapter 33

THOUGH I WAS TIRED the next morning, I still forced myself to go to church, partly because I had signed up to wash the coffee pots and the cups after fellowship hour. Ellie wandered into the kitchen as I was working and practically yelled, "There you are!" I almost dropped the pot I was scrubbing.

"Sorry, I didn't mean to startle you," she said.

"What makes you think you startled me? I mean besides jumping and nearly dropping this pot," I said, laughing. "I didn't realize anyone was still here."

"I looked for you and thought you'd already left, but I saw your car in the parking lot. Let me grab a towel and help you." I showed her where the towels were stored, and she pulled one from the shelf and unfolded it. "Goodness, these towels are ancient! I've never looked around closely in this kitchen. It could use an update!"

I laughed and replied, "Yes, I suppose it could. How are you doing after our long day yesterday?"

"Oh, I'm fine from the festival. I feel like I got a great night of sleep for the first time in ages, but I was looking for you today because the sermon hit me hard."

I nodded in understanding. "Forgiveness. It's not so easy for some of us."

"It felt like Reverend Peters was talking directly to me. As if he was trying to tell me something."

I finished washing the last pot, dried my hands, and said, "I think most of us should have been taking notes today. Struggling with forgiveness is a common problem."

"You don't think he was calling me out specifically?" she asked.

"No, I don't. Would you like to sit someplace so we could talk about it?"

"We're the only ones still here. Can we just sit in the fellowship area?"

We left the kitchen and walked into the fellowship area where there were chairs set up for people to sit and visit while they enjoyed their coffee. We found a couple of comfortable chairs and I decided to jump right into the conversation once we were settled. "Has the topic of forgiveness been on your mind lately?"

Ellie's eyes grew wide. "Yes. How did you know?"

"I've noticed in myself that when I reflect on the sermons that feel like they were meant for me, it's because they're about a topic I've already been thinking about. I thought the same might be true for you."

"I'm glad to know our pastor isn't a mind reader, but yes. Forgiveness has been on my mind. I'm working on it, but I'm still angry at Clark and I don't want to forgive him." She paused for a moment, reflecting. "Maybe what I actually mean is that I don't know how to forgive him when I'm still so angry."

I nodded. "Ellie, the first thing I need to say is that I'm not an expert on this. In fact, as I've been thinking about it lately, there are people I still need to forgive as well. Anything I say will be things I need to say to myself too."

"Lydia, you have a way of speaking that not only makes sense to me, but it helps me think things through. I want to hear what you have to say."

"The first thing I think we both need to hear is that forgiveness is more for our own benefit and well-being than for those we need to forgive. When you forgive Clark, it doesn't mean you're telling him you trust him, rely on him, or are reconciling with him. It's just that you forgive him. In some cases, I don't think you even need to tell the other person you have forgiven them. Again, it's about healing yourself. It seems that withholding forgiveness frequently means we haven't fully released the hurt we're still holding onto. When we forgive, we no longer carry the toxins and pain from the injury. We are laying the trauma down and saying it no longer has control over us."

"My anger has been a toxin. It's been eating me up. That's part of the reason I drank so much. I was trying to drown the anger."

"I understand trying to find something, anything, to drown out your pain, but it doesn't work, and now you know that." I paused because this next part was hard. At least, it was especially hard for me.

"Ellie, there's another part to forgiveness besides forgiving Clark."

"What?"

"We also need to forgive God for anything we blame Him for, and we need to forgive ourselves. I think we are often afraid to even admit that we blame God for something or for allowing things to happen. I mentioned before that I don't think God causes bad things to happen—they just do. But we sometimes still blame

God. Then, and this part is very hard, we also need to forgive ourselves.

"When we withhold forgiveness, we are focused on the other person's failings instead of acknowledging our own. We need to look at our pain and evaluate what, if any, part we had in that pain. Until we forgive the other person, I'm not sure we can acknowledge our part. We need to acknowledge our own part in the situation, if there is one, and then we must forgive ourselves too."

"I'm not sure I can do all of this!" she said.

"On your own, maybe not. But with God, you can. It's hard to believe that God loves us and forgives us when we haven't loved and forgiven ourselves. Remember too that you have friends and family who will help you. They are there to support you and help you work through this. Community is so important. You can't do it on your own."

After picking at a fingernail for a while, Ellie looked me straight in the eye. "And you're dealing with something like this too? Are you struggling with forgiving others and yourself?" she asked.

"Yes, I'm struggling with this too. We are on this road of forgiveness together, and God is with both of us."

She sighed. "You know, this isn't where I saw my life heading. This pain, this shame, I didn't see it coming. Maybe that's part of the anger too."

"So, then that is part of what needs forgiveness. We're human, Ellie. We have dreams and plans, and sometimes they don't work out the way we envisioned. All I know is that we can't keep carrying this pain. We need to work through it and then forgive. That is crucial in shedding the shame," I said.

"It's not going to be easy, is it?"

"Easy? No. Worth it? I absolutely believe so."

Ellie stood and said she needed to get home, and when I stood up from my chair, she hugged me. "Thank you for listening to me today. You've given me some things to think about. I will be praying that we can both forgive the people we need to. Including ourselves."

"And I will be praying for you too. We can do this."

Ellie blinked back tears as she hugged me again, and then she left. I went back into the kitchen to finish putting away all the dishes. I glanced around and thought the kitchen didn't look so bad, but as I held up a towel with holes in it, I admitted that maybe we did need an upgrade.

An inner voice questioned me as I drove home that afternoon. Who was I to give advice to someone else? Especially about forgiveness. I should have kept quiet since I was struggling too. I told the voice that I'd admitted to Ellie that I was also struggling with this topic.

I decided I would call Ellie in a few days to check on her. Perhaps we could have ongoing conversations to see how the other was doing. We could share what had gone well on our road to forgiveness and what we were still struggling with. It would be wonderful to have someone to talk to who was also working on the same problem.

I also decided to journal about forgiveness and my conversation with Ellie while it was fresh on my mind. But before I did that, I needed something to eat. Aunt Lu had decided to go out for lunch with a friend, so I made myself a sandwich. A thought occurred to me while I was eating, so I decided to call Gail. She picked up after the second ring.

"Hi, Gail," I said.

"Hi, Lydia! How are you?"

"I'm fine. I was thinking about you as I ate my lunch, so I thought I'd call this afternoon. What did you think of Reverend Peters sermon today?"

"It was powerful. Forgiveness is such an important topic. At least it's been an important part of my journey. What did you think?"

"I agree. I know it's something I still need to work on. In fact, I wondered if our small group should discuss it at some point."

"That's an excellent idea!" Gail said.

"Should we meet soon and discuss our upcoming plans, so we don't forget to add this topic?"

"Great minds think alike. I was going to ask you the same question."

After we settled on a time and marked our calendars, we ended the call and I went to my room to do some writing. I sat at my desk, pulled my journal out of the drawer, and paused to gather my thoughts.

My conversation with Ellie has caused me to contemplate forgiveness and my need to forgive. This will be hard, and I don't look forward to the task. I need to forgive others, and perhaps most importantly, myself. I wonder which will be the hardest. God has forgiven me, but it is hard to feel that in my soul since I have not fully forgiven myself yet. There are also times when shame creeps back into my life, and that makes forgiving myself extremely difficult.

I know I must forgive my rapist, but the pain I have felt since that horrible night has often been excruciating. How do I forgive someone who has caused me such deep pain? After all these years, I know he will never apologize to me. I'm sure he still doesn't think he did anything wrong. Besides, what I'm experiencing is my own pain. If I don't forgive him somehow, then this will continue to haunt my life.

A big part of my shame has always centered around my actions after the rape. Perhaps I need to objectively evaluate what happened and assess to what extent my own actions contributed to my pain and how much was actually caused by others.

I wonder if part of forgiveness is accepting that I'm human with human flaws. I've always wanted to be better than average. But in the end, I'm only human, and I need to accept that I can and will make mistakes. I think my actions after the rape were because I'm human. I was hurting, and I didn't know how to fix it.

It also occurs to me that forgiveness is important if I want to move forward. If I hold on to my wounds without forgiveness, then I am holding myself prisoner to the past. I don't want to be chained to it. The future looks too promising to be stuck in this forever.

I stopped writing as I remembered one of Grandmother's lessons. She had written that I needed to stop running from the past. She'd said that to fully live God's redemption, I needed to forgive myself and acknowledge that God had forgiven me. She also said I needed to realize how loved I was by others. I smiled and said out loud, "I remember your lessons, Grandmother. I'm trying to live them."

I told Ellie that I have often heard withholding forgiveness only hurts the person holding onto the pain. It seems that this harms me in several ways. It keeps me tied to a painful past and stops me from fully acknowledging and accepting God's redemption and love. And by playing these old recordings of shame, it is difficult to play new ones.

It is too painful to hold onto pain. It's time to focus on new recordings of redemption and love. I need to forgive. It is time.

I put my pen down. Forgiveness was going to be one of the hardest lessons I had faced since I had moved back home. It would take time and prayer, and I hoped Ellie would be willing to process this topic together. But for now, I needed a nap.

Chapter 34

I HAD A BUSY WORKDAY PLANNED, so I started tackling my to-do list early. I had clients I needed to talk to, and I knew I should try to reach a couple of them before they left for work. After those calls, I also realized I was behind on paperwork, so I spent a few hours tackling that too. The morning quickly turned into afternoon, and soon the afternoon was rushing by. Before I knew it, it was time to head to Gail's for dinner. She greeted me with a smile on her face when I arrived.

"I'm glad you're here," she said. "I just tried a new cookie recipe that I'm thinking of making for our next church fellowship event. Since your aunt is the best cook I know, you are the perfect judge."

"I think I'm a far second to Aunt Lu for judging cookies, but I'm happy to try one." Walking into her kitchen, my eyes grew wide as I looked at the stack of chocolate chip cookies on the platter. "Chocolate chip cookies are my favorite! And these are huge, so how can you go wrong?"

"Dinner is hot out of the oven. Let's eat that before you try one."

"Oh, Gail, life is short. Let's just try one cookie before we eat."

She laughed and nodded her approval.

After I had savored every crumb, I announced my judgment. "You need to share this recipe with me because Aunt Lu will love it."

"You think they're good?" she asked.

"No, I think they're delicious."

"According to the recipe, the key is making them larger like this. Don't ask me to explain the chemistry behind that, but they are tasty. I'm glad you liked it. Now I won't have to be embarrassed with some inferior cookie recipe. Maybe you can even write a testimonial that I can include with each one."

We sat down together and enjoyed a delicious baked pasta dish and a salad, making small talk as we ate. After we had put our dirty dishes in the dishwasher, I said, "Okay, now we need to get down to business and discuss the small group. Do you think we have covered everything we need to on the topic of being enough? I would love to say we could put some closure on it, but I'm guessing it's temporary. It always has a way of creeping up again."

"I agree. I think this is something that society keeps telling us about, so we will need to continue to discuss it as well. One piece that I don't think we've ever discussed is the importance of gratitude as it relates to being enough."

"I hadn't thought of those being related. How do they fit?"

"If we base our worth on money and possessions, we will never be satisfied, and we'll never believe we have enough. What most people truly want is a deep sense of contentment, and you can't experience that without first having a deep sense of gratitude. Along with gratitude is love—for God, others, and ourselves. I think, when we have gratitude and love, then we are at peace, and that helps us realize we have enough and that we are enough."

I nodded, letting Gail's ideas sink in. "Gratitude, love, and being enough. Previously, I think I would have separated those thoughts and not considered them as being so tightly woven together."

"I think it's often easier to separate our thoughts along these lines. It takes effort to make the different pieces fit together, but I think it's important that we do. We feel complete when we put the pieces together. And when we have gratitude for all that we have and are, we know we are enough. We aren't left wanting more because we are content."

"I agree, this would be good to share with the group," I said.

"I think we could have some good discussion on the topic. We could even challenge each other to write something down that we are grateful for each day. Remember, I struggled with low self-esteem and feelings of being unworthy for years, and I still must be careful not to slip back into that way of thinking. At one point in my life, I felt so poorly about myself that I only saw the negatives in my life. A therapist challenged me to write down one thing I was thankful for each day. I tried it only because I wanted to show her it was a stupid idea and wouldn't change anything, but I was wrong. Suddenly, where I once could see only negativity, I noticed beauty, kindness, and love. I saw positivity in abundance. When we force ourselves to think about something, it often encourages our brains to keep thinking in that way."

I looked at my friend with awe. She had turned a simple assignment from a therapist into a new view on life. "That sounds like an amazing exercise. I know I often take things for granted and don't appreciate all my blessings. I'd like to see how discussing gratitude and focusing on it would help me with my own feelings of being enough. Maybe we can tackle forgiveness after we cover gratitude."

My mind was going in multiple directions. It was important that we share this with our group. I also wondered what impact it would have if more people realized they are enough and that they are loved just as they are.

We continued to make notes until we fell silent for a while. Then I looked at the plate of cookies on the table and said, "Why yes, Gail, I believe I would like another cookie." I chuckled as I grabbed one and bit into it.

"And I would love to join you in having another one too," she said, taking her own from the plate.

Our serious conversation was over for the evening, and we laughed and talked about what television shows we had watched lately and what books we had enjoyed. It was good to have a friend to laugh with and who I could also discuss serious subjects with too. I was so glad I had found Gail. She wasn't afraid to listen to difficult conversations. I realized that our friendship would be the first entry on my gratitude list.

Chapter 35

AS WAS THE CASE ON MANY MORNINGS, I awoke with my brain racing. My thoughts rambled from being enough to offering forgiveness. I hoped to find some clarity about these ideas for myself, and that they would be helpful for Ellie and the other women in our small group. My thoughts followed me downstairs and into the kitchen.

"Good morning, Aunt Lu. Is the coffee ready?" I yawned.

"Oh my. It's that kind of morning, is it?" she said.

"Yes. I thought I slept okay, but I don't feel like it," I told her.

"You're in luck. There is still plenty in the pot. And there are muffins too. After some nourishment, would you feel like checking the orchard to see if there are any ripe apples out there yet? Our early variety should be ready about now. It always seems I'm up to my elbows in apple sauce at this time of year."

"After a muffin and some coffee, I'll be good. I'll take a couple of buckets with me just in case."

I thought that fresh air and time in the orchard were just what I needed. I was tired of thinking, and I just wanted to be. Letting go of my deep thoughts and doing some physical work instead sounded like a good plan.

I grabbed a few buckets and a ladder and headed out after I'd finished my coffee. When I reached the orchard, I was amazed at all the ripe apples I saw. I had my work cut out for me. And even after I picked them all, Aunt Lu and I still had to deal with them. While we typically used this kind only to make apple sauce, I wondered how they would taste in a pie. Thoughts of warm apple pie encouraged me to get busy.

My brain kicked into gear while I worked. Though I was hoping that a physical task would cause my brain to take a break, my soul clearly had a different agenda. After all, my soul knew this was where I was most open to revelations.

I knew from experience that my brain would not let go until I'd dealt with these thoughts, so I let my mind wander where it wanted to go. Not surprisingly, it landed on forgiveness again. I knew I still had work to do. I had confronted my trauma and discarded the shame and all the pain that accompanied it. But I still hadn't forgiven.

I dropped another apple into the bucket and paused for a short break, looking out across the acres of fields.

Was I honestly ready to offer the forgiveness I needed to give? I took a deep breath and told myself that I was. I thought about the pain I had experienced in my life: losing my parents when I was a child, then losing my beloved grandfather when I was in junior high, and the horrible, life-changing date rape and all the bad relationships I had after that. I had experienced immense pain in my life, and I vowed to evaluate it all, the parts that were not my fault and the parts that were.

I moved on to another tree and looked up at the ripe fruit waiting to be plucked. Fond memories of picking apples from these trees with my grandfather flooded my mind. I remembered pointing out a ripe apple near the top of the tree once and telling him we couldn't pick that one because it was so high up that it was almost to heaven. He shocked me when he climbed the branches and grabbed it. I looked at him with awe and shock once he climbed down again, but he winked and told me we didn't need to tell Grandmother about picking that one.

I missed my grandparents and my parents, and I knew I always would. My parents' deaths were tragic events. Over the years, I had felt anger surrounding their deaths. It took years to understand that my anger was part of my grief, and it took a long time to process those feelings. Though the pain and loss would always be with me, my faith told me that in some way, I would one day be reunited with them.

I bit my lip, bracing myself for what I did not want to face but what I knew had to be confronted. Gently, I dropped the apples I'd just picked into the buckets and then sat under the tree I'd been harvesting. I took another deep breath and held it, then blew it out slowly. It was time to address the night I was raped.

Society continues to tell survivors that rape is their fault or that they could have taken some action to stop it. This has led me and other survivors to struggle with guilt and shame. After all these years, somewhere deep inside, I still blamed myself.

Once again, tears came to my eyes. This time, I felt a nudge telling me it was time to say unequivocally that the rape was not my fault. I was not responsible for this pain. Going out on a date was not bad, and I wasn't a bad person for being there. I was not responsible for his bad actions.

Rape is not the survivor's fault.

My rape was not my fault.

I leaned my back into the tree and wept. My body trembled with the power of that statement. Those six simple words struck me to my core. They were the most powerful and cleansing thing

I'd ever told myself. *My rape was not my fault.* Somewhere deep inside me, I had refused to believe it. Perhaps it was too painful to believe that I had no control over that act of violence, or perhaps the voices of society that blamed me, the survivor, were too loud to ignore. I had listened to those voices for what seemed like a lifetime, telling me that good girls wouldn't have been in that situation. And good girls would have fought.

I finally accepted that those voices were wrong! And now I knew in my soul that my rape was not my fault. After all those years, I truly believed it. Though I didn't need to forgive myself for the rape itself, I did need to forgive myself for how long it took me to seek help and confront my pain.

A loving and compassionate voice deep inside me said, *You are forgiven, loved one. Facing trauma takes time and patience, and what is important is you've faced it now.* Forgiveness washed over me. I sat in that holy moment for several minutes. I had waited years for this forgiveness, and I didn't want to rush it.

When I was ready to move on, my thoughts turned to forgiving my rapist. I didn't have the energy to do that yet, but all things in time. And besides, I still had apples to pick. Today's breakthrough was a good start.

I stood up again and looked at all the ripe apples left on the trees. Where did they all suddenly come from? It seemed there were more left to be picked than when I began. I needed help to complete this job. While I couldn't pick all the apples by myself, I decided I would focus on finishing the tree I had been sitting under. I moved the ladder closer to where I needed it and then climbed up to the top. It took no time at all to fill my bucket. As I assessed the tree, I knew the only way to reach the rest of the apples was to climb high into the branches. I smiled again at the memory of my grandfather doing the same thing, and then I started climbing. When I reached the next limb above me, I made the mistake of looking down. What was I thinking climbing this high with no one around? Those last apples would need to wait. I carefully climbed back down again and sighed with relief when my feet were on the ground. My heart was racing, so I sat down to relax.

As I rested, I remembered what followed the rape. The list of my poor choices seemed endless, and I regretted the relationships I had entered. I began to forgive myself because I had been vulnerable and naïve. I was trying to heal something that I knew was broken, but at the time, I didn't know how to heal it. I had built such a wall to protect myself that I couldn't hear God telling me I was loved, and I interpreted the silence as a rejection from Him instead. It had taken me a long time to understand that I was only human and that God loves me unconditionally. And since I was only human, I was allowed to forgive myself for all the mistakes I had made, including using coping mechanisms that made the pain worse. Although I suspected the guys I dated knew I was vulnerable and took advantage of that, I forgave them because I knew I needed to do that for my well-being.

I sat for a few more minutes, reflecting on the work of forgiveness and realized I was exhausted, though I wasn't sure if it was from picking apples or from forgiving. On the hard days that would surely come, when the words of the world were loud, I would need to remember this day. I had forgiven myself for what needed to be forgiven, and I had realized in my soul that my rape was not my fault. I didn't often tell myself this, but I was proud of my hard work.

Soon, I heard someone pull into the driveway. I slowly stood up again, and my body reminded me of the physical work I had done. But my aching muscles were quickly forgotten when I saw Sam's truck parked by the house. I yelled to him that I was in the orchard and waved him over.

"Hi, Sam. What are you doing here so early?"

"I just wanted to see my favorite person," he said. Then he looked at the full baskets and added, "Wow! You've been busy! Want to take a break? We can walk around the farm to see all the beautiful flowers."

"That's a great idea! I always love admiring all their beauty."

Though Sam was very knowledgeable about farming, he admitted he'd never paid attention to the flowers. I pointed out a few of my favorites. I also showed him an area where some of the flowers had not survived and told him my ideas about what I wanted to plant next.

Eventually, Sam stopped and looked at me. "I have a confession to make. I stopped by because I did want to see you, but I also wanted to talk to you about Ellie. I'm a bit concerned again. She's been very quiet the last few days. I'm wondering if she's backsliding and may start drinking again."

My mind raced. What should I share? He was her brother, but Ellie hadn't given me permission to share the details of our conversations. Sam watched me carefully. I must have taken too long to respond because he started jumping to conclusions.

"I'm right, aren't I?" he asked. "You don't want to say anything because you know I'm right and you're concerned too."

"No, that's not it. She and I have talked, but I'm trying to decide what I can share without breaking an unwritten confidence. She didn't tell me not to talk to you, but she didn't say I could, either."

"So, everything is fine?"

I paused again. Could I truthfully answer that she was? I wasn't sure. She and I were both looking into the dark corners of our lives, trying to forgive both those who had hurt us and ourselves. This was hard, exhausting work. I could understand if she started drinking again. How could I answer Sam's concerns?

I took his hand and looked him directly in the eyes. "I think she is okay, but quietly keep an eye on her. If you're convinced she is drinking again, be sure to let me know. She is processing some difficult things right now."

I took a deep breath as I realized I should share with Sam what I was processing.

"I should also tell you that I'm on another difficult journey myself. Reverend Peters's sermon about forgiveness struck a chord with me, and I realized I have people I still need to forgive, including myself. To do that, I must face some painful realities again. It's hard to do, but I know I need to do it to move beyond my brokenness. I've been making good process."

Sam nodded. "I'm sure Ellie needs to do this too. I'm not sure how she can forgive Clark, but I know she needs to forgive herself for the things she's blamed herself for."

This man was so wise. We started walking again and ended up in the apple orchard. And then Sam suddenly stopped again and took both of my hands in his.

"Lydia, I hope you know that the rape was not your fault." He paused for a minute and then said, "As far as how you reacted afterward, you need to forgive yourself for being human and making mistakes. God loves you just the way you are." He paused, and I thought I saw a single tear in his eyes. "And I love you too."

I knew in my heart that he was sincere, but I also knew I was still scared. I decided I needed to be honest.

"I care about you deeply. At this moment, I'm a little scared to call it love. As you know, my track record with relationships is dismal, and I'm afraid. Would you be willing to stick with me a little longer as I learn that our relationship can be different from those in my past?" I asked.

"Yes, I will wait. If you promise to keep working on forgiving, then I promise to be beside you and support you in your journey."

I looked at him in awe and found myself speechless. His willingness to support me while I continued to heal was amazing. How could I respond? I hugged him and thanked him for his patience.

"I've made some true progress on forgiving myself. Just like you said, I'm only human, and I've forgiven myself for that. I've also forgiven myself for how long it's taken me to face my trauma and process it. I do still have others to forgive, but I promise to keep working on that."

He took my hand, and we walked back up to the house. I'm not sure what we talked about because I couldn't stop thinking about Sam saying he loved me and that he would stay with me as I worked on myself. I now had another entry idea for my gratitude list. I knew I was truly blessed.

Chapter 36

It had been several days since Sam had shared his new concerns about Ellie, so I decided to call and invite her over for coffee. To my surprise, she said it was her turn to play hostess. We made plans for Saturday morning.

When I arrived, Ellie invited me in and told me my timing was perfect because her coffee cake was almost done. The timer went off just as we entered the kitchen.

"See. Perfect timing," she said.

I breathed in deeply and smiled. "I smell cinnamon. I love cinnamon."

"Ah, I'm glad to hear that. Sam and Jordyn both love this recipe. I was hoping you would too. You know, it's a little intimidating cooking for you since you live with such an amazing cook."

"You're not the first person to say that. I am blessed though. One of these days, she needs to try teaching me how to cook. She finds such joy in cooking for others, but I know the day will come when I will need to fend for myself."

"Or, when you will want to cook for yourself *and* someone else."

I almost choked on my coffee. "Oh? What makes you say that?"

Ellie's laugh was instant. "Oh, Lydia. You and Sam are the worst-kept secret around here. I've seen how the two of you look at each other. And I noticed how comfortable you were together when we went to the music festival. I even saw him put his arm around you."

"No one has said anything to me, so I'm a bit surprised. What are people saying?" What I really wanted to ask about what she thought of our situation. I couldn't bring myself to voice the words.

Ellie brought the coffee cake to the table and put it on a hot pad. Then she smiled and said, "Everyone is happy for both of you. And I do mean everyone. That includes me."

Relief flooded through me. I had been concerned that our relationship might be difficult for her.

"I'm so glad to hear that. I wasn't sure what you would think," I admitted.

"I'm thrilled. Truly. I just pray that Sam doesn't mess this up. He's so shy, and he has only dated a few women."

"I'm praying that I don't mess this up either. My track record with relationships is rather dismal."

"You and I are working on fresh starts, and that means with relationships too," she reassured me.

"I will try to remember that to help push my fears aside."

Ellie cut the coffee cake and served me a piece. Once she'd served herself, she said, "Now, I'd like to change the subject. How do I know when I'm done forgiving?"

I nodded. "I struggle with that too. I strongly believe we may need to circle back to all of this in the future. These old feelings and voices sneak back in, and we will have to remind ourselves that we have forgiven ourselves and others. But I think that we are on our way to healing when we stop denying our shame, stop running, and face the trauma."

"I must confess, it is difficult to forgive Clark. He keeps telling me how worthless I am and what a horrible mother, wife, and person I am. It's like he reinforces my worst thoughts about myself, and he causes me to doubt everything."

Anger flared within me, but as calmly as I could, I said, "He's a critic, and that's what critics do. They point out our worst fears and cause us to doubt ourselves. Something I've recently realized is that the problem isn't with the critic. It's that we believe the critic instead of what God tells us. We need to constantly remind ourselves to listen to God. God says we are made in His image, and that means we are enough, and we are loved. God is who we should look to anytime we are doubting our worth. That's what we need to hold onto."

Ellie smiled. "That's beautiful. Yes. That's what I need to hold onto."

"Remember this too: When Clark is being his nastiest, his actions are about himself. They aren't about you. They are about his wounds and his pain."

Ellie sat quietly and reflected. "I hadn't thought about it like that. I think that makes it easier to forgive him."

"Yes. And remember, we have wounds and pain as well. So that should help us in forgiving ourselves."

Ellie reached over and grasped my hand. "Thank you for sharing all of this with me."

"You're welcome. I'm glad we are on this forgiveness journey together."

We sat quietly, enjoying our time together and sipping our

coffee. Then eventually, Ellie said, "I need to start working on lunch. Would you like to stay? Sam might enjoy this nice surprise."

"I'd love to stay. What can I do to help?"

"Would you be willing to cut up some fruit? I'm going to throw hamburgers on the grill. I already cut up some veggies."

"Consider it done," I told her.

Right on cue at noon, Sam walked in the door. The look on his face when he saw Ellie and me putting lunch on the table was wonderful. He was obviously surprised, but he also seemed at peace with it. "Where's Jordyn?" he asked. "If she was here, then all my favorite people would be at the table with me."

Ellie and I smiled at each other, and we all sat down together.

Chapter 37

OUR SMALL GROUP DECIDED to take a break for a few weeks since so many people were taking summer trips. At our last gathering before the break, Gail and I decided to ask members to share something from our time together, if they wanted to—perhaps something they had learned or a memory they cherished.

Gail started our discussion. "I want to thank everyone for their faithful attendance and willingness to share. I also want to say how wonderful it's been that we honor each other and treat everyone with respect. Unfortunately, I've been part of groups where competition, pettiness, and judgment made the experience less than pleasant, but this group has been the complete opposite. Our time together has been very special to me."

Sarah was the first to speak. "I'm so thankful for all of you. Your support helped me survive these difficult months. When I lost my job, I thought I was worthless. It seemed that my entire purpose in life was taken from me. Our conversations and your support have shown me I don't need a specific job or career to be complete."

Several of us nodded in response. It was wonderful to hear Sarah's words. She had been very quiet during the last few meetings, so I didn't know how she was processing this challenge.

Then she smiled and added, "And although I don't need a job

to feel complete, I do need one to provide food and shelter for myself. I'm thrilled to announce that I have another job interview next week."

Gail said, "Oh, that's great news, Sarah! We will all be praying for you."

Everyone nodded and added their words of congratulations before we moved on.

Anna was the next to share. "I echo what Sarah said. I'm so thankful for each of you. I know I may say something different in the fall when I send my baby off to college, but today, I'm feeling more secure in who I am. I appreciate all of you reminding me that I am enough because I am made in God's image. That has been so comforting to me. It's still been hard, but I keep coming back to that. Now, just remind me of this again when fall arrives."

I replied, "We're here for you today, and we will still be here for you in the fall."

Ellie decided to share something as well. "I guess I should have brought an entire box of tissues tonight. My emotions seem to be boiling up to the surface. I honestly don't know where I would be without all of you. The last few months have been so difficult. I think I've felt every negative emotion there is. My divorce is the hardest thing I've ever faced, but you have been with me through it all. When I'm challenged with thinking there is something wrong with me or that I'm worthless, I keep going back to the idea that I'm one of God's beloved. And every time I remember that, I feel at peace. Then I remember that I'm enough and I can face the next day. You are all my angels here on earth."

I searched for a tissue in my purse. After I found one, I dabbed my eyes and blew my nose. Then I looked at Gail. I was so glad we were close enough friends that she knew I just couldn't speak. Gail knew she needed to close out the evening.

"Friends, we have been on an amazing journey together this year. When we first gathered, I doubt any of us expected to go through the ordeals we have faced or that we would become so close. Here's one last topic before we leave tonight. I've recently been thinking about how we tend to compartmentalize our lives. We separate ourselves into little pieces or buckets. It might be our roles that we separate, or we might compartmentalize our emotions. Regardless, we divide them off because we don't think we can bring them all together and process them. I, however, think we need to integrate ourselves to be whole and complete. We need to bring all our roles, pain, and emotions together and process everything as one complete woman. It's hard work, but in truth, that is what we have all been doing. Am I enough as I am? Am I enough with all the pain and hardship I'm facing? Am I enough no matter what role I'm currently in or not in at all? This is challenging, but I think we are beginning to see it's worth the effort. Because when we are whole and complete, we are also content and full of joy. And when we are content and full of joy, we can handle all life brings to us.

"And how do we do this? How do we become whole and complete? It's just what several of you have said this evening— accepting and believing that we are enough because we are made in God's image. And when we know we are enough, we see things in a new way. So, remember, you are whole and complete because you are made in God's image, and you are enough. In fact, you are more than enough. You are beloved. Thank you for blessing my life, and I can't wait to begin our group again in a few weeks."

Conversations continued as the group was not anxious to end the gathering. It was an emotional and impactful meeting that was difficult to leave. Eventually, everyone left, and Gail and I tidied the room. As we cleaned, Gail asked me how I was doing.

"These women amaze me. Not only because of what they have been through and are still going through but because of their bravery in sharing it with all of us. It's made me wonder if God has put these amazing women in front of me to give me courage to share about my battles. I don't have answers yet, but I need to pray about it. I liked what you said about being whole and complete. I'm not sure I'm there yet, but I know I'm closer than I was."

"You are indeed, my friend. I think it is wonderful and brave that you are wondering if God is calling you to share your story. That's between you and God, but I love that you have acknowledged that possibility. And now, I need to go. I still have some last-minute packing to do for my trip."

I gave Gail a hug and wished her safe travels on her vacation. My drive home found me appreciating the small group even more. It was wonderful how supportive everyone was toward each other. I also considered Gail's comments about compartmentalizing. I recognized myself in her description of separating the parts of our lives into different buckets. I also realized that another part of compartmentalizing was allowing others to set expectations for us and to define us as someone other than who we were meant to be. When that happens, we end up living a divided life of a false self and our true self. We are not living as the people God designed us to be. I had allowed society's expectations to define me in the past, and it caused me a great deal of pain. It was impossible for me to find the peace I was seeking when I was living that way.

Gail was correct, integrating ourselves was hard work, but it was worth it. I was so thankful that none of us were alone on this journey. We had each other, and God was with us each step of the way.

Chapter 38

I HAD FINALLY COMPLETED my training with the domestic violence and sexual assault support center, and it was now time for me to work solo with my first survivor, Liza. My role was to ensure she never felt alone as she made her way through the challenging legal process. I would even be in the courtroom to support her. Although the training was extensive, and as an attorney I was certainly aware of the legal process, I was nervous. I needed to push aside my own memories and feelings and focus on the woman I was there to assist. Our first meeting was to discuss the legal process and what that would entail for her.

On the day of our meeting, Liza walked in and sized me up immediately. I recognized the look of someone who didn't trust the person sitting across the table from her. I started to panic a little. How could I help this woman whose expression seemed to be saying *I don't trust you*? But then I stopped as I realized my old thoughts were coming back to me. My defense mechanisms were in high gear, and I had quickly put up my own wall so that Liza couldn't see my own pain, fear, or trauma. I took a deep breath and jumped in.

"Liza, my name is Lydia. I'm here to support you and advocate for you during the legal process. I know you don't know me, and you may be nervous about this process, but I want you to know that I am here for you and will help you in any way I can. You can trust me to have your best interests as my only focus, and I will be with you through the entire trial. You won't be alone. You have an ally."

"I thought you were just some social worker or attorney that was assigned to me," she said.

"I am an attorney, but I'm not serving in that role here. Today, I'm a volunteer who is here to be a support person for you."

She nodded that she understood and sat down across from me at the table. We then discussed her case and how it would move through the judicial system. As we went over the details, she began to cry. "I'm not even sure it was rape. I thought he loved me," she said.

"Just because you thought he loved you doesn't mean this wasn't rape," I explained.

We sat quietly for a few minutes. I didn't want to rush the conversation and cause her discomfort to increase. When her tears subsided, she told me we could continue. We talked about the specifics of what to expect. Liza doubted whether she could handle the pain. She talked about her fears that no one would believe her and about the horrible shame she felt. I then reminded her she wasn't alone.

"Do you think you can face what you are feeling if I'm there sitting in the front row? You can focus on me while you are testifying," I told her.

"I should do this for other women, shouldn't I? So maybe he won't do this again?" she asked.

"That could be one way of thinking about this. But I also think there is another reason. I think you should do this for yourself, to stand up and say this was wrong. To say that I may be the victim of a crime, but I will not live as a victim. To say, I'm a survivor. I'm strong enough to stand up and say you will not have power over me again."

Between her sobs, Liza said she would move forward with the court case and that together, we would face this.

A couple of weeks later, it was time for the trial. The cross-examination was difficult for Liza, and she broke down on the stand. The judge called for a brief break so she could compose herself. I met her as she stepped away from the bench, so I could walk with her out to the hallway. Her rapist stood up quickly as he stared at me and loudly said, "I know who you are. I know Clark, and I was at the bar one night when he told the bartender about you. He said you thought you were this powerful attorney when you were actually just a tramp. He also said you turned his wife against him. And now, isn't this something? Two pieces of trash are here, trying to damage another innocent man."

I tensed up. Clark had indeed followed through on his threat and told more people about my past. My emotions flashed from anger to fear to horror to shame and then back to anger. My typical response to a verbal attack was to lash out and to unleash my quick wit and sharp tongue, but as I began to react, this man in front of me suddenly changed. My soul suddenly saw him as a wounded child of God like me. I didn't know what caused his woundedness or what caused him to act in violent ways, but I knew he was also a child of God. That did not excuse his behavior, and he still needed to be held accountable. But he was also broken and a child of God, and I needed to acknowledge that too. I took a few steps toward him so that I would not need to speak loudly to be heard.

"I know you don't believe that," I said. "I sense that you are a wounded person, and I'm sorry for your pain." Then I escorted Liza out to the hallway.

Outside the courtroom, Liza finally found her voice. "How could you say that to him? Especially after what he did to me and what he said about the two of us."

"I'm not sure I can explain this because I'm surprised myself," I replied. "That wasn't how I was going to respond at first. You need to know that I believe he needs to be held accountable for his actions, but I also sensed that he is a broken person living in pain. I don't know if I'm allowed to tell you this, but I'm going to anyway. I am also a rape survivor. It's taken me a very long time to even admit it. I have carried my pain and trauma for years. So, you see, I am also an injured person, and I know what pain feels and looks like. I was able to see this man as a wounded person. I hope that makes sense, and I hope you know I didn't say it to cause you pain. Seeing him as a wounded person may have been the most difficult thing I have ever done, but it was freeing. If I can see him as a child of God, then I can see myself as a child of God too.

"When court resumes, you need to tell your story. You also need to know that no matter what happens in that courtroom today, you are also a child of God. There are rules of law that must be followed, so I don't know what decisions the judge will make. But you will have calmly stated what happened, and you will go home knowing you didn't hide your story. I hope that all makes sense, Liza. All I know is that I believe you, and I know that God is grieving your pain with you because He loves you and you are one of His beloved."

Liza just stared at me, unblinking. "Well, you just unloaded a whole lot of church on me all at once. I don't know what to think or what to believe, but I hear the sincerity in your voice. I don't know about thinking about him as a wounded person, but I guess I can view him as a person."

"If you see him as a person, you can start to take your power back. You are strong enough to say what happened, and you are strong enough not to let him have that power over you anymore. I know you will have to keep reminding yourself of this, but you're taking the first step toward healing."

"Are you preaching to me or to yourself?" she asked.

I smiled. Liza could see right into me. Maybe it was because we shared a common trauma. "I'm speaking to both of us. I wish I'd had the courage to do what you are doing now. I spent too many years being afraid and too many years living in shame."

Liza paced in the hallway, and I could tell she was thinking things over. "I'm loved and I'm one of God's beloved. I'm not sure, but I think that means something to me. Thank you. I will have to think about whether I believe that creep in there is wounded too, but I do have the courage to continue."

"You are a brave woman, and you should be proud of yourself. No matter what happens next, you are enough," I said.

Liza nodded, and we went back into the courtroom. The judge reconvened the trial a few minutes later, and Liza was back on the stand telling her story. She did a great job of keeping her composure. She never wavered on what happened. Unfortunately, as is often the case, the judge ruled that there was not enough evidence for a conviction. Liza bowed her head and shed a few tears when the verdict was announced. I gave her a hug and reminded her that she had stood up to her bully and that made her victorious, regardless of the verdict. She nodded and whispered to me, "I am enough, Lydia. I am enough."

"Yes, you are. You are most definitely enough."

I was pleased that the accused exited the courtroom without acknowledging either of us. In fact, he never lifted his head. It was even clearer to me now that in some way, he was in pain. Liza noticed it too. After he left the courtroom, she whispered again. "You know, you might be right about him being in pain. Did you see the way he left? He looked like he'd lost. And the judge ruled for him."

"Our brokenness comes out in all different ways," I said.

"This was an awful experience, but I am so glad you were here with me. Thank you for sharing your experience and letting me know the real you. I appreciate your time and your support. Can I give you another hug?"

"You bet you can." We hugged and then I told her, "Life will probably still be hard for a while. If you start to struggle in any way, please reach out to the center. We offer a wide variety of help. And I'll be in touch over the next few weeks just to make sure you are okay."

Liza nodded in understanding. "That would be great. Thanks again. Would you mind walking with me out to my car? I don't want to risk running into him on my way out."

"I absolutely will go with you."

When we made it to her car, I gave her one last reminder. "Remember, anything you need, be sure to call." I handed her another business card. She thanked me and drove away.

I was now alone with my thoughts. Sadness and anger came over me. It was times like this when I became frustrated with the law. I wondered how the judge didn't see the truth and believe there was enough evidence. Somehow, by the time I reached my car, I felt peace replacing my anger. It seemed that Liza understood that rape was never the fault of the survivor. She seemed to be handling things as well as could be expected, but I would be sure to check in with her to make sure that was true going forward.

I thought about how her rapist appeared to me as wounded, and I realized how caught off guard I was with my reaction to this idea. I had initially wanted to lash out at him for his horrible actions and mean-spirited words. But instead, something deep inside of me recognized him as a wounded child of God. My thoughts then turned to my own rapist. I didn't know if he was wounded or not, but I admitted that he was also a child of God. For that reason and for my own well-being, I forgave him. Not just in words, but in my soul.

Once again, I found myself in powerful, cleansing tears. Forgiving him released me from the power of the hurt he had caused me. I knew I would occasionally flash back to that horrible experience, and some days the pain would sneak back in, but I also knew that I would always have this day of forgiveness and freedom to reflect upon.

Chapter 39

WHEN I PULLED INTO THE FARM after my day in court with Liza, the familiar sight of Sam's truck parked by the shed made me smile. Instead of going into the house, I went to find him first. I was delighted to find not only Sam, but Jordyn as well. Sam was busy working on the riding lawn mower, and Jordyn looked very bored.

"Hi, you two. This looks like quite the project."

Sam looked up and said, "Hi, Lydia. I'm not sure how much longer I can keep this old mower working. You may want to start looking for a new one."

"It's certainly had a long life. It's probably time. Jordyn, what are you up to?"

"Nothing," she grumbled.

Sam looked over at her. "I thought you wanted to see Lydia."

"Yeah. Maybe."

"Well, Jordyn, you're in luck. I've been inside all day, and I would love to take a long walk. Sam, can you spare your niece while we do that?"

This time he didn't look up from his work. "Yup. Take your time. I'm going to be working on this for a while."

As we left the shed, I said, "I need to take my purse and bag into the house. Why don't you come with me, and we'll see if we can find some nourishment for our excursion?"

Jordyn flashed a smile and responded, "That sounds great!"

When we went inside, I called out to Aunt Lu that I was home. I heard her call out from the living room. "Hi, Lydia! I'm in here watching my program."

"Just wanted you to know I'm home, but Jordyn and I are going for a walk," I told her.

I heard Aunt Lu sit up in her recliner. "Jordyn's here? Well, wait just a minute. I have something special for her to try." Aunt Lu met us in the kitchen. "When you told me about Gail trying a new recipe, it inspired me to be creative. I used my favorite oatmeal raisin cookie recipe, but instead of just plain raisins, I added chocolate-covered ones instead." She handed us each a cookie. I could tell from Jordyn's face that oatmeal raisin was not her favorite. I decided to quickly try mine, and I couldn't believe how amazing my first bite was.

"Okay, Aunt Lu, I must confess, oatmeal raisin cookies aren't my favorite, but these are amazing. Please tell me that they're good for me because they have raisins in them."

Aunt Lu chuckled. "Of course they are. If you overlook all the butter and sugar in there."

Jordyn decided to try hers too. She took a bite and smiled. "I'm with Lydia. I usually don't like oatmeal raisin, but these are good."

"Let that prove a person is never too old to be creative. Now, since I have two thumbs up, I'm going back to watch my show."

"Thank you for letting me try one of these cookies," Jordyn said.

"You're welcome, honey. Maybe you should take one with you in case you get hungry. Lydia will walk the calories off you."

Jordyn smiled. "Thank you. I think I might do that."

We both took Aunt Lu's suggestion and grabbed an extra cookie to go. I also filled two water bottles. "Okay. Ready, Jordyn?"

She held up her cookie, smiled, and replied, "I think I have everything I need."

As we walked outside, I wondered if I should ask Jordyn why she wanted to see me. I was afraid that would put her on the defensive, so instead, I began with a generic conversation starter. "How have your summer activities been so far?"

She shrugged. "Fine, I guess. Nothing too exciting."

"I'm trying to remember what all you've done. I seem to remember you went to a sports camp."

"Yeah. I went to a two-week camp and played soccer, volleyball, and basketball. None of my friends went, so it was just okay."

"Are you taking music lessons over summer break?" I asked.

"Yeah."

This was going nowhere, so I decided we should just walk. We finally made it to the creek, and I told Jordyn I wanted to sit on the big rock and rest for a few minutes. I thought maybe just sitting and staring at the water would let her relax if she wanted to talk. I was correct.

After a few minutes, Jordyn asked, "Lydia, how do you make a boy like you?"

That was not what I was expecting to hear. I thought for a moment and then said, "Well, truthfully, I'm not sure you can."

"Oh. I was afraid of that," she said.

"Do you want to talk about this?" I asked gently.

"So, there's this boy, and I thought he liked me. He even told me he did, but now he doesn't." She stopped talking and turned to look at me. Tears filled her eyes, and she didn't try to hide them. "It seems like nobody likes me. I'm not pretty enough. I'm not thin enough. I'm just . . .not enough for anyone."

Her emotions were palpable. "First, can I give you a hug?" I asked.

Jordyn nodded her agreement. The entire time I hugged her, I prayed. *God, help me know what to say. Help me to say something that will help ease her pain and not cause harm.*

"I have so many thoughts going through my head. I don't know if any of it will make sense or help, but I hope some of it will. First, please know that what you are feeling is common, especially at your age. That might not help you feel better, but maybe knowing you're not alone will help a little. Also, I want you to know that I like you. In fact, I love you, and I know your parents and Sam do too. But I also know it hurts to think that no boys like you. I know what it's like to think you aren't thin enough or pretty enough, because I've felt that way too. But I've recently realized that we are all enough just the way we are."

Jordyn sniffled. "You think so?" she asked.

"I know so. Now, this is important. Don't fall into the trap of doing something you don't really want to because you think that's what you have to do to make someone like you. It doesn't work, and it just ends up making you feel worse. Don't try to be someone you're not. You don't need a boyfriend to be enough. You are enough just the way you are, just the way you look. I know that's hard to believe right now. It's even hard for adults to believe, but it's true. Maybe you could focus on friends that you enjoy being with. That's the point of relationships. To spend time with people you enjoy."

Jordyn was silent for so long that I wondered if I'd rambled on too much. Finally, I took a deep breath and started talking again. "I know I've shared a lot, but this is an important issue for me. Trust me, I made countless mistakes trying to make people like me when I was younger. I tried to be someone I wasn't, hoping that someone would like me. Unfortunately, it just caused me pain."

Jordyn stood and looked at me with her mouth hanging open. Then she said, "I can't decide if I want to yell at you for all of that or hug you or laugh because I can't believe you went on and on like that."

I beat her to the laughing part. "Oh, I'm so sorry. When I'm passionate about something, I can't stop myself."

"I've learned that now."

I laughed again. "Okay, but seriously, did you hear me? You are loved. And it doesn't matter what society tries to tell you. You are enough just as you are."

"This is a lot. I don't know what to think," she said.

"Yeah, I threw quite a bit out there. Just remember this one thing. You don't *need* to have a boyfriend to be enough or be complete. And everything else I said, well, we'll talk about it again another time. But slower. And maybe only one idea at a time."

"That's a deal. But I do have one question."

"What's that?"

"You said I don't need a boyfriend. Does that go for you too?"

"That's right. It does."

"And you said a relationship should be with someone you enjoy spending time with."

"That's right."

Jordyn's smile filled her face. "So does that mean you enjoy spending time with Uncle Sam?"

"I wondered where you were going with this. So, you know, huh?" I smiled.

"Yup, I do."

"You're right. We do enjoy spending time with each other. It took me years to realize that it was better to wait for someone I enjoyed being with than to date the wrong people."

"I'm glad you found each other. And I guess if it took you this long to find each other, then I have plenty of time."

I put my arm around her shoulders as we headed back to the house. "All the time in the world, Jordyn. Good things can't be rushed."

Chapter 40

SUMMER SEEMED TO BE WINDING DOWN. Some mornings brought a cool wind that hinted at fall's upcoming arrival. I loved autumn, but I didn't want this summer to end. It was wonderful to spend time with Jordyn. Sam and I had also been able to spend a considerable amount of time together, and I knew the changing seasons meant he would soon need to work nonstop. Indeed, I had enjoyed this summer immensely.

It had also been a time of growth and reflection for both Ellie and me. We had met a few more times to discuss forgiveness and lovingly pushed each other when we thought the other hadn't gone far enough or had slipped backward in our growth. Although it was difficult to forgive those who had hurt us, we discovered it was extremely difficult to forgive ourselves.

And even though I had spent a great deal of time thinking and praying about forgiveness, I wasn't ready for the sermon that Reverend Peters preached on Luke 7:36–50. That was the story of Jesus forgiving the town harlot. As was my custom, I read the scripture before church. When I read those verses, I immediately felt the old feelings of shame and anxiety creep in. I remembered the sermon that Ellie thought was meant just for her. Simply thinking about a sermon based on these verses in Luke filled me with the same fears. Would Clark show up and yell that the town harlot was sitting there in church? Deep down, I knew that wouldn't happen, and so I stepped beyond my fear and went to church. Besides, what reason would I give to Aunt Lu? *Oh, I can't go to church because I'm afraid someone will call me out in front of the congregation as the town harlot.* Rationally, I knew it would just be my own uncomfortable memories and voices that I would need to face.

I became increasingly nervous as I sat through the service. Finally, it was time for the sermon.

"I have preached a couple of sermons over the last few months regarding forgiveness," Reverent Peters began. "They have centered around why we should forgive others and ourselves. Perhaps I should have started with the power that comes from God's forgiveness. But as I was reading chapter seven in Luke, I was reminded of that. Jesus was invited to the home of one of the Pharisees. While he was there, the town harlot learned of Jesus's presence, and she crashed the party. This was very risky behavior for her. Pharisees stoned women like her, but she crashed the party anyway. She went directly to Jesus and fell at His feet, and then she washed his feet with her tears. Stop and think about the number of tears it would take to wash someone's feet. I think it would be accurate to say she was sobbing. Then, she dried his feet with her hair and anointed them with expensive perfume.

"Do you remember what happened next? The Pharisee was not happy that this woman with a bad reputation was in his house. But then, Jesus told him a story of two people, each with a debt that was forgiven. Jesus asked, which person would be more grateful, the person with a small debt or the person with a large debt? The Pharisee answered, the person with the larger debt. Then Jesus pointed out that this woman was forgiven for her numerous sins. She cried tears of gratefulness. Tears of joy. Jesus told her that her faith had saved her and to go in peace. He didn't need to tell her to go and sin no more. Her tears tell us that she was done being the town harlot. These were tears of joy. Tears of salvation. Tears of her own resurrection. She had been wearing the garments of pain and shame, but she left that house wearing new garments, the garments of God's love and redemption."

I didn't hear the rest of the sermon. I was too focused on thinking about the gift this woman had received and her reaction to it. Even though others viewed her as a harlot, she was still loved by God. The Pharisee only looked at her past, and he had a limiting belief that she would always be a harlot. But that's not how Jesus viewed her. Jesus viewed her as a child of God, and that belief changed her life.

As I reflected on what this woman must have felt, I remembered the scripture about Jesus's baptism. I wished I could've been at the water's edge so I could have seen Jesus come up from the water. Then I would have heard God's voice from heaven say, 'This is my beloved, with whom I am well pleased.'

Once again, I remembered what the author Henri Nouwen had said. He believed that the words Jesus had heard were meant for all of us. That meant the town harlot was also God's beloved and that He was also pleased with her. I took a deep breath because finally, I knew in my soul that this was meant for me too. Those words had been impactful when I first heard them. I had thought of them often, but now I knew and felt their truth in my soul. They had made the long journey from knowing them in my head to believing them in my soul. God was telling me, *Lydia, you are also my beloved. And in you, I am well pleased.* They had finally become alive and had blossomed inside me.

Perhaps the reason this impacted me so deeply was because I'd spent my life trying to prove to others and to myself that I really was enough. I'd spent my life seeking but never feeling that I had achieved affirmation, acceptance, and love. And yet, I had always had that from God. I did nothing to earn it but simply be. God didn't care about my career or my appearance or what happened in my past. God loved me just as I was. Yes, I finally knew it in my soul: in me, God was well pleased. And because God loved me and was pleased, I was enough. I had been searching for something, but what I really needed was God's blessed assurance. It was never missing, although before that moment, I had not completely understood or accepted that I had always been enough in God's eyes. Perhaps understanding and accepting these truths should have been obvious to me, but it wasn't. I had to face my trauma before I could feel God's assurance.

I may be the woman who was raped and then led a life full of bad decisions, but I was still enough. My shame had made me feel unlovable, but God had always loved me. And sitting there, surrounded by my faith community, I absorbed the truth of God's love and grace that made me whole and complete. And Ellie, Jordyn, Anna, and Sarah were enough too, even amid everything they were facing. God's message was true for everyone. We were all loved and affirmed.

I had felt God's love during my spiritual transformation over the last year, but this was different. It felt stronger. Perhaps it was the difference between accepting God's love and knowing in my soul that I was more than loved. I was beloved.

Critics and society and my own inner voices might try to make me forget who God created me to be, but God's message was clear. I would work hard to discard my old beliefs of shame and inadequacy by playing God's message over those old voices in my mind. It would be a journey, but I had God and this wonderful faith community to travel with me.

I sat as if I was in a trance. I was barely aware of anyone sitting around me. Then, Aunt Lu touched my arm and handed me a hymnal that was opened to the final hymn for the day. The piano and the voices of the congregation floated around me, but I didn't really hear the words because the title of the song hit me. "Just As I Am." As the congregation sang, I closed my eyes and focused on the words I heard God whispering to me. *That's how God loves me. Just as I am.* It had taken time and prayer, but I finally knew that truth in my soul.

Sam wrapped his arm around me, and I opened my eyes and realized he was looking at me with concern. I gave him a reassuring smile and put my arm around him too. I whispered, "Just as I am. That's how God loves me."

Sam smiled back. "Yes, it is, Lydia."

As I put my hymnal back in the rack, Reverend Peters gave the closing blessing. "And may the God of love and peace be with you today and every day. Amen."

I breathed in deeply and thanked God for that love and peace and for helping me believe that I *was* beloved and enough, just as I am.

Dear readers,

If you are interested in using this book for a small group or book club, please go to my website *letawrites.com* for suggested study questions.

About the Author

Leta Buhrmann was born and raised in Central Illinois. Even though she still calls Central Illinois home, she has been on a multi-year journey. This excursion has not added mileage to her car but instead has been a spiritual journey, called by God to explore the dark corners of shame and the pain of trauma. This journey then led her to know in her heart that God's grace and love are for everyone, and she feels called to use her writing to share that news with others.

Leta and her husband have been blessed with two daughters and their families, plus one "grand-horse," and one "grand-kitty."